13 MONSTERS

ERIC S BROWN

SEVERED PRESS
HOBART TASMANIA

13 MONSTERS

Copyright © 2021 Eric S Brown

WWW.SEVEREDPRESS.COM

ISBN: 978-1-922551-07-8

13 MONSTERS

"It's coming back!" Flynn screamed as something in the water splashed violently near the far end of the tunnel they were wading through.

Corporal Peter Anthony held his position to Flynn's right as Barrett moved hastily between and passed them. The glowing, blue hot flame of his thrower's igniter drew Anthony's eyes to it in the dim, flickering red emergency lighting within the tunnel. Barrett's weapon wasn't standard issue. They'd picked it up from what appeared to be an emergency, mini-cache of weapons inside the Drake complex. Barrett raised up the flamethrower's barrel and let loose. A blazing burst of fire, so wide that it filled the tunnel from side to side ahead of them, exploded outward from its nozzle. Anthony knew the fire wouldn't do any real damage to the monster they were up against but it sure as hell scared the thing enough to keep it back. It could have easily come zooming in at them below the waterline but instead kept its distance. He didn't know if it was the light or the heat or both that bothered the creature and didn't fragging care so long as the flames kept the thing at bay.

The fourth member of their squad, Cody, was behind them, his M27 clutched in white knuckled hands. None of them were really trained for this crap. It was one thing to charge in guns blazing and rescue people from terrorists . . . dealing with things like the creature ahead of them was something else altogether.

The geyser of flame spewing from Barrett's flamethrower sputtered and died.

"I'm out," Barrett warned, retreating towards where Cody stood.

"Guess we're up then, huh?" Flynn tried to quip but the fear in his voice was so thick that it stifled the wittiness of what he had said.

The creature came spiraling through the water like a guided missile targeting them. Its body rolled completely over, twisting continuously like an otter that was showing off might, picking up speed as it came. Corporal Anthony hated to label the thing a sea serpent but it sure as hell wasn't an oarfish. This thing was nearly twenty feet long with eyes that glowed red beneath the water. Its body was long and thin, covered in armor-like scales. And a mouthful of razor teeth that gleamed when it splashed upwards out of the water with its jaw unhinging like a snake's appeared too as it struck. Anthony had always thought of sea serpents as massive things, monsters that sunk ships, so maybe this thing was a sea snake or something. He sure hadn't ever seen or heard of anything like it existing in real life before coming face to face with this creature.

Flynn cried out, flinging himself to the left, attempting to dodge the creature's attack but the snake was too fast. Its teeth plunged through the light armor of his vest, sinking into the flesh that it was supposed to protect. Water splashed as the snake thing's impact knocked Flynn over backwards. He disappeared below the waterline along with the snake. They were thrashing about beneath the churning water, the snake coiling around him. Anthony stood helpless. He couldn't take a shot at the creature without almost certainly hitting Flynn too. Though Anthony hated it, he knew what had to be done. . . cut their losses and run while they could. It went against everything he believed as a Marine but there were hundreds of people depending on them, people who had no other chance of getting out of this complex and off this island alive.

"Run for it!" Corporal Anthony yelled, motioning at the distant airlock at the other end of the corridor. The water was almost waist high so moving through it wasn't an easy thing. The rest of the squad followed after him as he waded hurriedly towards the airlock. Barrett had shrugged his flamethrower from his shoulders and left it behind. Now empty, it served no purpose and would only weigh him down. Cody came splashing along behind him, panting and pale. The kid was new to their squad. Anthony couldn't blame Cody for being freaked out. Hell, he was too. Anthony was a pro though. His view of things was if it bled, it could be killed and that had seemed to work out well so far since they'd arrived in this nightmarish hell hole.

Anthony slowed, letting Barrett and Cody pass him. He stood looking back at where Flynn had been taken under by the snake creature. There was blood in the water. Anthony knew it was Flynn's. It had to be. The water was calm again. Anthony didn't see any sign of the snake creature. He sucked in a breath, steeling his nerves. The thing could be anywhere beneath the water's surface, slinking along the bottom of the tunnel towards him. His grip on his M27 grew tighter as sweat ran down over the lines of his forehead from beneath the edge of his helmet. Anthony knew he had to do something or he'd be next.

Taking one hand off his M27, Anthony snatched a grenade out of his vest, removing its pin. Tossing it into the water, he turned and sprinted up the tunnel towards where Cody was still trying to get the airlock door to open as Barrett covered him. Barrett saw Anthony coming and what he had done.

"Fire in the hole!" Barrett yelled, slamming Cody against the airlock door, with his body blocking the younger private from the force of the blast exploding behind Anthony.

Anthony grunted as the shockwave from the grenade picked him up, flinging him forward into the water. The explosion had knocked the breath from his lungs and they burned as he held his breath long enough to scramble back up out of the water. Gasping for air, Anthony heard something click inside the thick metal of the airlock. It slid open, Cody pretty much toppling through it, pushed by the water that surged past and around him. The corridor beyond the airlock hadn't been flooded like the one they were in though it was lit by the same flicking red of the emergency backup lights. Barrett was shoved in by the water too. He caught himself on the edge of the airlock door though and kept his balance. Barrett motioned for him to hurry the hell up as Anthony fell into the now rushing water so that he could swim rather than try to run, splashing frantically toward the open doorway.

Barrett's M27 swung up, targeting something behind him. Anthony glanced over his shoulder and saw the snake creature. It sped through the water, silvery scales breaking the surface every few seconds as its body spun like an incoming torpedo. Anthony picked up his own speed as Barrett's M27 roared, letting loose on full auto. The rounds that missed the creature zipped into the water, vanishing beneath it. Those that found their target sparked against the creature's armor-like scales, bouncing harmlessly away.

Anthony let the current of the water flooding into the corridor that the tunnel led into carry him the last of the way as Barrett moved aside to allow him through. Cody, who had recovered from the sudden rush of water pushing him into the corridor, sprang over to the airlock door's controls. His fingers danced over the keys there and the door slammed shut, nearly closing on Barrett.

Barrett cursed loudly, glaring at Cody, as Anthony hurled himself up to his feet. The corridor they were in now stretched out into the distance and the water that had rushed in had spread out. It wasn't even up to the tops of their boots anymore and was lowering with each passing heartbeat.

"Let it go, man!" Anthony ordered Barrett before he could do anything stupid. If Cody hadn't closed the airlock door when he had, they'd still be engaged with the monstrous thing that was on the other side of it.

As if to prove his point, the airlock door shook in its frame as the creature smashed against it. The sound of the impact reverberated down the corridor around them. The door didn't give though. Anthony

figured it was strong enough to keep that thing out. .
.at least for a while.

"We left Flynn out there!" Cody wailed.

"He's dead," Anthony grunted. "That thing tore
him apart."

"So much for the no one left behind bit huh, sir?"
Barrett grumbled, clearly just as ticked with him as
he was with Cody.

"Frag it, Barrett. You saw that thing," Anthony
growled. "There was no stopping it and the lives of
the people we're here to save come first."

"Copy that," Barrett nodded, seeming to calm
some after being reminded of their objective.

"What now?" Cody asked. "We sure as hell can't
go back that way."

"Nope," Anthony agreed looking at the sealed
airlock door then turning his gaze to look down the
corridor they had entered. "We've got to find a way
back up to the surface though so we keep moving and
hope we catch a break, maybe find a terminal you
can use to tell us exactly where we are so we can get
our bearings."

"Yes sir," Cody's head bobbed up and down.

"Barrett, you've got point," Anthony ordered.

****

Matt Drake's hands worked, adjusting his tie, as
he stared at himself in the tall mirror mounted on the
wall of his bedroom. He cut a rather dashing figure.

His body was lean and not too soft, hair midnight black, and eyes a sharp green. Having turned twenty-eight only a couple of months back, the amount of power and money Matt had amassed in that short span of years was more than impressive. It was simply staggering. His breakthroughs in the biotech industry had been as lucrative as they were revolutionary. A smile slid over Matt's lips as he finished with his tie and stood up straighter. Growing up, he had always been the odd man out, the nerd who got his head shoved in boys' room, or worse. Now, he was one of the richest young men on the planet.

A low groan from his bed told Matt that one of his escorts from the night before was stirring. On the left side, tangled up in the blankets, was a redhead while on the other side of the bed, a blonde was sprawled, one of her legs almost dangling over its side. Both women were naked and very attractive. They had served as his entertainment last night to take the edge off the day that lay ahead of him. Matt didn't care which of them was waking up. He had no use for either of them this morning. There was work to be done and his staff could attend to whatever needs the two women might have. He walked briskly out of the bedroom and found Lewis waiting for him in the hallway beyond its door.

"Good afternoon, sir," Lewis was beaming. The mop of wild, brown hair atop his head as poofy as ever. "I trust your night went well."

"Afternoon?" Matt asked, raising an eyebrow.

"Yes sir," Lewis assured him. "It's shortly past noon I am afraid. Shall I send someone to attend to your . . . company. . .from last night?"

Matt grunted, ignoring Lewis' question, getting straight to much more important business. "Is everything in place for this evening?"

"You need not worry," Lewis huffed, sounding somewhat offended. "The few things which still need to be attended to will be finished well ahead of the arrival of your guests."

For all his power and money, Matt didn't really have friends or family. Sometimes he thought that they were merely things that lesser souls held onto to make themselves feel as if they had value. Matt held himself aloft from the majority of people in the world and his parents were both dead before he was twenty. Still, if he were to consider anyone a friend, it would be Lewis. The man had served him well for the last seven years, anticipating his needs and keeping his secrets. Lewis was the singular person Matt truly trusted. Without Lewis, Matt knew just how more trying his life would be.

"Right," Matt said. "I should've known you would be on top of things, Lewis. Perhaps I just need some. . ."

Before Matt could finish his sentence, a servant came rushing around the corner of the hallway with a cup of steaming black coffee. Lewis smirked at him as Matt took the coffee from the servant's hands and sent the man scurrying away.

"Thank you," Matt chuckled, nodding at Lewis.

"My pleasure as always, sir. Such things are what you pay me so handsomely for," Lewis laughed.

Matt sipped at his coffee as he and Lewis walked towards the stairwell that led down to the mansion's main floor. It burnt his tongue but Matt needed the caffeine more than he wanted to admit.

"And our latest acquisition?" Matt asked.

"Settling in nicely," Lewis grinned. "Properly sedated and ready for display tonight."

"Good," Matt smiled. This latest addition to his collection was so massive it couldn't be housed inside the massive complex beneath the island. Its holding cell was below the complex and almost as large as the island itself. Gathering his collection had at times put Matt on the brink of bankruptcy despite the profits from his medical breakthroughs. He'd spent numerous years and hundreds of billions locating and capturing the creatures that would be put on display tonight for the elite, rich, powerful, and famous of the circles he was forced to deal in to see.

The Octa was the 13^{thth} creature to be added to his collection and it was Matt's pride and joy for more reasons than just its size and rarity. It was perhaps the only surviving member of its species and so ancient it could easily be considered to be the closest thing on the Earth to an immortal.

Thirteen was Matt's lucky number and as thus he had decided it was time to show off what he had gathered beneath the island to those that were worthy of beholding them. Of course, each person attending his showing would be required to sign nondisclosure papers and there would be no media present. Matt had given Lewis clear orders in that regard. Any journalists who came poking around tonight were to be summarily dealt with and their careers ravaged.

Matt was excited and as giddy as a child on Christmas morning though he was doing a fantastic job of hiding it. No one else had likely even conceived of assembling a collection along the lines of his much less been able to accomplish it. Much of his breakthrough had been brought about by the creatures of his collection. The depths of Earth's oceans were far less explored than outer space and only Matt knew their deepest and darkest beauties and secrets.

Lewis stepped off the stairs onto the mansion's main floor, heading straight for the room that was supposedly Matt's office but was really a personal monitoring station. It was a place where Matt could view and watch the creatures that were his without descending into the heavily secured complex below. Only Lewis and himself had the access code to the keypad that controlled the "office's" door. Lewis keyed in the code and the door unlocked. As they entered, the room's lights turned on. They were bright and harsh to Matt. He raised a hand to shield his eyes while they adjusted.

"I know you'll be wanting some time alone, sir," Lewis said. "I'll leave you to it."

Lewis left the room, closing the door after him.

Matt took a seat behind the room's desk. Across from it, the wall wasn't covered in monitors but rather was composed of multiple screens, each of which showed one of the containment cells of his collection. There were more than thirteen screens with the extras displaying different angles of observation of those same cells. He stretched, leaning back in his chair, the smile on his face growing wider. Tonight belonged to him. For the first time, he'd show the world what money, power, and determination could truly achieve. It was more than being famous or owning things like your own island.

He'd never given his island a name, only the complex under it and that name had come more from those who worked there than himself. The Drake complex was home to more than three dozen scientists, staff, and security personnel. It ran the entire length of the island and extended downward. Above ground, the island was fairly simple. In its center was the mansion Matt called home. Around it were several smaller homes assigned to both the mansion's staff and some of the staff. There were two landing pads, one on each side of the island, for helicopters and VTOL craft as a full scale dock on its northern side. His guests tonight were being flown in a luxury VTOL and were slated to arrive just after sunset. Matt shook his head. He thought of most of them as fools and the rest merely as tools which had to be cared for in order to preserve business relationships that kept his monstrous income continuing to flow into his bank account. Still, tonight, he was going to blow their minds and fill each and every one of them with awe. . . and perhaps a trace of terror.

****

Deep inside the Drake Complex, Dr. Harrelson was finishing up with the last preparations that were required for the evening's "show and tell". There was a scowl upon his face as he keyed in the order for the sedatives to be released into containment cell five. An image of the corridor outside of the cell filled the screen of his work station. Reggie and Powell were at the cell's entrance. Despite the regulations, Powell was puffing on a thick cigar, his graying hair poking out from under his uniform, worker's cap at random spots. Harrelson could have used the complex's intercom system and railed the older man out for it but knew there was no point. He'd just catch Powell doing it again next week. The man was addicted to the filthy things and had no intention of kicking his habit. At least Reggie was competent at his job. In truth, Reggie was the best of the entire six member security force. The kid was a former special ops. trooper, who even at his young age had seen more action than the others combined. Dr. Harrelson had pleaded with Mr. Drake to promote Reggie to being the head of the complex's security numerous times but that position was held by Captain Rachel Sheeran and would likely be until something went horribly wrong within the complex or she grew tired of the position and left on her own. He had no personal beef with Rachel. She did a well enough job with everything except keeping her personnel in line at times. The drunken parties of the security staff were infamous and Rachel didn't give a crap about minor regulations such as the one that Powell was violating now.

The monitor showing the interior of cell five went dark. Dr. Harrelson sighed, leaning over to hit the intercom button.

"Reggie," Dr. Harrelson called out, "Do you have eyes on our guests?"

He saw Reggie glance around at the camera on the wall behind him and then back into containment cell five before responding. Powell was cursing under his breath as he stabbed his fat cigar out against the wall of the corridor.

"That's a negative, Doc," Reggie reported.

"Everything's gone dark inside the cell."

Dr. Harrelson watched the feed coming in from a camera mounted on the corridor's wall, nervously, as Reggie cautiously backed away from the thick glass of the cell. Rationally, Harrelson knew that was no reason to be worried. Even if the creatures within containment cell five were making some sort of play, its glass was nigh unbreakable. The things had been held inside the cell for over a year now and had not come anywhere close to shattering their way out. Still, a bad feeling crept over him. Reggie was frowning too and that creeped him out even more.

"You lose the feed from in there, Doc?" Powell grumbled, walking over to the cell to rap the knuckles of his right hand against its glass. "I wouldn't worry about it. Those things have trashed cameras before."

Turning his chair slightly, Dr. Harrelson's fingers danced over the keys of his station's control board, quickly running not only a system check but an overall check of containment cell five. His eyes bugged as he read the data that scrolled before his eyes across the smaller screen of his station. The PH and other aspects of the cell's water were all out of whack. His mind raced to find an explanation for what he was seeing and couldn't. The readings looked more like those of containment cell seven where the Charon, The creature in containment cell seven was named after the Bathochordaeus Charon, which was a form of giant Larvacean, though in reality it had nothing in common with them except for its almost completely transparent appearance. No, the thing in cell seven had much more in common with the creature from the old horror film, The Blob. The Charon was nearly invisible to the naked eye in the water and preyed on anything composed of meat and flesh that came near it. Capable of being both a liquid and solid, the Charon was hard to defend against. The creature could shape its form however it needed. Once getting a hold on its prey, the Charon killed with bio-chemicals that could burn through the strongest metals. Why would the readings on the water in cell five be . . .?

Dr. Harrelson went pale, his heart skipping a beat inside his chest.

"Reggie! Powell! Get out of there!" Dr. Harrelson yelled over the intercom. "Now!"

Without warning, the glass of containment cell five seemed to give way. Water exploded out of the hole, pouring into the corridor. Reggie was already running up the corridor, trying to escape it. Powell had been caught in the horizonal geyser bursting out of the cell. It slammed him into the wall, knocking his breath from his lungs in a pained grunt. Dr. Harrelson watched helpless to help either of them. The cell's emergency systems sprang into action, slamming down a thick metal plate over the rupture in its glass. The water stopped spraying into the corridor though it was already partially flooded. With the airlocks at either end of the corridor still sealed, the water was up to the mid point of Powell's chest as he stood up in it. Reggie had reached the left airlock and was looking back at Powell as if wondering what to do.

"You okay?" Reggie shouted.

"Fine," Powell huffed. "Just got the wind knocked out of me. What in the devil freaking happened?"

Powell's angry, questioning glare was directed upwards at the camera Dr. Harrelson was watching them through.

Dr. Harrelson didn't have an explanation. "You guys just get out of there. We can figure it out after you're both safe."

"No can do, Doc," Reggie said. "With the water in here, the airlock doors are locked down. You'll have to override one of them for us."

"I can do that," Dr. Harrelson nodded though he knew neither of them could see him. A flicker of movement on the screen caught his eye, drawing his attention. As Dr. Harrelson turned his head fully back towards the image of the corridor, he saw what seemed to be the water itself rising up behind Powell, who didn't seem to be noticing it at all.

"Powell!" Reggie yelled.

Dr. Harrelson saw that Reggie had drawn his

sidearm and was splashing through the water towards Powell.

The older man turned around to find himself facing a mass of water that towered over him. It came down over Powell like a crashing wave. As it passed over him, Powell's flesh bubbled and dissolved, leaving exposed white bones gleaming in the harsh lights of the corridor.

Realizing at once what he'd just seen, Dr. Harrelson's fingers started flying over the controls of his console, unlocking the airlock behind Reggie.

"Reggie!" he screamed. "It's the Charon! Powell's dead! Get the hell out of there!"

Stopping roughly in the water as it churned around him from his momentum, Reggie froze where he was. From where he was, Reggie could see Powell's bones moving about beneath the surface of the water. The Charon had them with its grip. The older man's skeleton was breaking apart and beginning to dissolve like his flesh had. Reggie whirled about, heading once again for the left airlock door.

Dr. Harrelson had finished overriding the airlock's emergency lockdown mode and it swooshed open. A surge of water burst through, carrying Reggie along with it. Dr. Harrelson stabbed a button to close the airlock. Its door slammed back into a locked position. Reggie scrambled to his feet on the other side, getting the hell out of the water that had come with him into the next section of corridor. A worker in that section came running towards him.

"What's going on?" the woman shouted. "Are you okay?"

Reggie waved her off, motioning for her to keep back. He was staring at the water that covered the floor around his feet, making sure, as best he could, that the Charon wasn't hiding in it. After a moment, Reggie's gaze shifted to the closest security camera.

Dr. Harrelson noticed. He was still watching the security officer. Powell was dead. A lot of questions were about to be asked of him and Harrelson didn't have any answers.

****

Matt Drake came storming into the conference room. Reggie, Dr. Harrelson, Captain Rachel Sheeran, and Director Smith were gathered there, sitting around the room's only table. Lewis wasn't with him. Matt couldn't afford to take Lewis away from the projects he was already handling. Cheeks flushed red from anger and frustration told everyone else in the room that he wasn't in a mood to be trifled with.

"Anyone want to tell me what the hell happened?" Matt barked as he punched the top of the table with a clenched fist.

"We. . .We don't exactly . . ." Dr. Harrelson began.

"You don't know?" Matt raged, glaring at the doctor. Harrelson seemed to sink into the white cloth of his lab coat. "Then just what the hell am I paying all of you for?"

"What happened should have been impossible," Director Smith said. "Each of the containment cells is separated and spread out to avoid things like this."

"Clearly it's not impossible," Matt huffed.

"I lost one of my men today." Rachel stood up, leaning onto palms that were pressed against the table top. "Do you even care about that?"

Matt cocked his head at her. "Don't," he warned coldly.

Reggie noticed Rachel hadn't said a "good" man or anything like that. Everyone at the table knew just what a jerk Powell could be. Still, he was a human being and his life had been brought to an end.

Matt returned his attention to Director Smith. "This is on you regardless so I fragging well want to know what happened and right now."

Unlike most of the others at the table, Smith didn't so much as flinch at Matt's fury. He sat with a calm expression, hands clasped together, lying in front of him.

"I understand how important tonight is to you, sir," Director Smith said, "but even so, I don't have all the answers. No one does at this point. From what we can tell so far, the Charon burnt through the complex walls and into containment cell five."

"How is that possible?" Matt demanded.

Director Smith shrugged. "The Charon is apparently much more intelligent than we originally believed. During the time we've had the creature in containment, it appears to have very discreetly been working towards such an escape from cell seven."

"And we didn't pick up any signs of the Charon doing that?" Matt's head snapped back around towards Dr. Harrelson.

"No," Director Smith said firmly, defending the doctor. "We did not. You have to remember when these creatures were brought in for containment here, in most cases, we were learning about them and exactly how to contain them from day one. We've done our best. Frankly, we've worked some minor miracles. Eventually though, something like this was bound to happen."

"And where is the Charon now?" Matt asked.

"It appears to have vanished back into the depths of containment cell five," Rachel answered before Director Smith could.

Matt looked sickened at her answer. "And my Mermen?"

"The good news is that the Charon hasn't eaten them all," Director Smith frowned.

"How many?" Matt's voice was sad and frigid.

"Slightly over half of them are missing, sir . . . at least from the count we've been able to get from the security feed coming out of the cell," Dr. Harrelson answered.

Before Matt could explode on the doctor, Smith butted in again to save him.

"Those missing Mermen could simply be in hiding. They are very bright creatures, Mr. Drake and could have sensed the Charon's presence in their cell, taking cover before the thing was able to attack them. Just because we haven't gotten visual confirmation on them yet doesn't mean that they're dead."

Matt ran his fingers up through his hair, veins bulging on his forehead.

"I want the Charon located A.S.A.P and back where it belongs," Matt said sternly. "And I want both it and whatever are left of my Mermen ready for tonight. Do I make myself clear?"

"Crystal," Director Smith and Rachel answered together.

"And after tonight is over with, I expect both of you to ensure that something like this never happens again," Matt finished and stormed out of the room.

Reggie looked at Director Smith and then Rachel. "That went well."

"Actually, it did," Rachel said. "For a moment there, I thought he was going to ask for my sidearm and shoot one of us in the head."

Scary as it was, Reggie could see she was serious. Such were the job risks when you worked for someone as powerful and rich as Drake was. .

.especially when the job was as remote as this one. Drake could easily have claimed any one of them died in an accident and that would have been that.

"Now that he's been dealt with, where do we stand on finding the Charon and the missing Mermen?" Director Smith asked Dr. Harrelson and Rachel.

"My people are overseeing the workers who are repairing the damage done to containment cell five right now. I should have a full progress report within the hour," Rachel answered. "So far, the Mermen have left them alone."

"I haven't been able to locate the Charon at all with the complex's sensors or cameras," Dr. Harrelson shrugged. "However, I believe the creature has retreated back into the Mermen's cell which could very well explain the lack of any attack on the workers."

"We need to make sure of that," Rachel blurted out. "That thing is dangerous and not just to the creatures in the containment cells. The Charon will eat anyone it comes across not to mention the damage that thing could do to the complex itself. If it eats through the wrong chunk of . . ."

"I am well aware of the danger we're in until the Charon is located," Director Smith nodded. "I prefer to believe that Dr. Harrelson's assumption about the thing retreating into cell five is correct. It makes sense though it does need to be confirmed."

"Are all of you forgetting how many people are

arriving on this island in a few hours?" Reggie butted in.

"Reggie!" Rachel snapped.

"I understand your concerns on that front," Director Smith sighed. "However, if we seal off both containment cells five and seven, Mr. Drake's guests should be perfectly safe while they are here."

"Assuming the Charon doesn't burn its way to. . ." Reggie started.

"That will be enough, young man," Director Smith stopped him. "We're all going to do what we can and it will be enough."

"Yes sir," Reggie grunted.

"Dr. Harrelson, I want you and your staff to drop everything, other than finishing up with the preparations for tonight, and find me the Charon," Director Smith frowned. "With the amount of money Drake dumped into this place's internal sensors, that should certainly be possible."

Director Smith took a deep breath and turned to Rachel. "Of course, I will want your people searching for that thing too."

"I'll put everyone I have on it as soon as the repairs to cell five are finished," Rachel promised. "But Reggie, myself, and Chuck will get started checking out the other corridors and cells visually right now."

"Good," Director Smith managed a smile. "We've all got our jobs to do so let's be about it then."

****

Klaxons blared throughout the U.S.S. Safeguard. She was the first commissioned ship of her new class, a mix of a rescue vessel and a destroyer. With a crew of thirty Navy personnel and three squads of Marines, her job was to head directly into hot zones and extract personnel trapped within them. She was like a Blackhawk of the oceans.

The alarm jerked Sergeant David Neil out of his dreams. He sat straight up in his bunk, banging his head against the bottom of the one above it. Cursing, he shoved himself up and hurried to get into his combat gear. He knew things must have gone to hell on that rich bastard's island if the Safeguard was moving in. She, along with her sister ships, the Rescue and the Redeemer, had been sent in days ahead of time by an undisclosed higher up in the Navy to watch over the island. Neil thought it was crazy, wasteful, and just plain stupid to invest so much and the efforts of so many men and women to ensure the safety of some rich guy and his employees. Nobody could be that important.

Neil looked around and saw that the others in his squad were rushing out the door to the mustering area. He grunted, gritting his teeth. Age must be getting to him. He was in his later thirties, about to turn forty, while the rest of his squad were still kids in their twenties. There was no hope of catching up to them but rank had its privileges. Neil had earned being late if he wanted. He finished getting geared up and headed for the rallying area.

"Sergeant," Higgs greeted him gruffly as Neil came walking in.

There were four squads all standing at attention in the rallying bay of the Safeguard, a mix of vets and newbies. Each and every one of them was suited up in combat gear. Some carried standard issue M27s while others were carrying weapons of their own choosing. Neil knew all their names though not all of them personally.

"Higgs," Neil acknowledged the NCO who was his second in command. He spotted Corporal Anthony standing with his squad. Anthony was a dang fine trooper and Neil was glad to have him.

Neil moved to stand in front of the gathered squads. "Okay, boys and girls, what we have here is a real load of crap. Something on that island has knocked out the place's main power grid and has put the lives of everyone on it at risk. From what I've been deemed worthy of being told, that something is a collection of dangerous sea life that the fragger who owns the island has been collecting and was showing off for the first time tonight. Our job is to go in and make sure everyone who is still alive over there stays that way. Any questions?"

No one spoke up. Neil nodded with a slight grunt of approval. "Then let's move, people!"

Moments later the M22 Osprey, carrying all four

squads, lifted off from the main deck of the USS Safeguard. Most of the Marines were strapped into seats in the VTOL craft's rear but Neil and Higgs stood in its control room, behind the two pilots flying it.

The weather had taken a foul turn after night had fallen. Winds whipped through the air and waves of rain fell from the sky. A bout of turbulence struck the Osprey. Captain Kennedy grimaced as the plane shook but managed to keep anything bad from happening. His copilot, Jones, looked worried.

"The weather's getting pretty choppy, sir," Jones commented.

"Nothing we can't handle," Kennedy replied. "Though this will likely be a bumpy ride for you and your boys, Sergeant."

Neil snorted. "Most of us have seen worse. You just worry about getting us there in one piece, Captain. That's all that matters."

"Thank God this place has a landing pad," Jones said.

Giving Jones a questioning glance, Neil asked, "You know this place?"

"We got briefed just like you did," Captain Kennedy smiled, "But I thought everyone knew about Drake Island. The guy's pretty famous."

Neil looked over at Higgs who simply shrugged.

"Don't tell me you've never heard of Matt Drake?" Jones blinked, real surprise on his face.

"Guess we don't get out much," Higgs answered gruffly.

"Who is this Drake guy?" Neil asked. "The only thing we were told about him is that he's the owner of this place."

"Matt Drake is a freaking genius," Jones laughed. "The guy's still young and he's one of the richest and most powerful people in the world. Made his name by creating medicines that have dominated the big pharma markets, everything from things to slow down aging to better treatment options for cancer and such."

Well, that explains why we're here, Neil thought. The whole world came down to money and power when you really looked at things. If some suburb in New York erupted into a war zone, it'd take a while to get real help to it but a guy like Drake apparently had three ships on standby tonight. That begged the question as to whether Drake was expecting trouble or if someone else had been. Neil supposed it didn't matter. His men were riding into danger either way.

"From the rumors I heard," Captain Kennedy began but was forced to pause and make a course correction due to the weather before he could continue, "Mr. Drake was supposed to have a hell of a lot of important guests tonight: celebs, rich folks, even some of our own higher ups."

"Figures," Higgs said gruffly.

"Doesn't it though," Neil agreed. "Some rich kid

makes a mess and we're sent in to clean it up."

Captain Kennedy refrained from commenting on what was being said by the two of them. Instead, he said, "We're on final approach to the island's VTOL pad now. E.T.A in three."

"Roger that," Sergeant Neil nodded. "We'll be ready."

Neil and Higgs headed into the rear of the plane where the squads under their command were.

"Head's up, people!" Higgs barked. "It's about to be showtime!"

The M22 Osprey came in hard as it touched down, jostling everyone aboard it. Neil was just grateful to be on the ground. The weather was only getting worse. The craft's massive blades were still spinning, roaring above them, as he and Higgs led the four squads out its rear door. As soon as the last man was off, the M22 rose back into the night sky. Neil glanced up to watch it being hammered by the winds and hoped Captain Kennedy could get the bird safely returned to the deck of the Safeguard.

"Sir!" Higgs yelled at him. The wind was so intense that Neil almost couldn't hear the NCO.

Across from the landing pad was the main gate of the Drake mansion. Neil motioned for Corporal Anthony and his squad to take point and for Higgs and his men to bring up the rear. No one had to tell the Marines they needed to hurry. The troopers sprinted to and through the gate, heading for the mansion, eager to escape the growing fury of the storm.

As the four squads reached the mansion, Neil held his own back. He signaled for Higgs to take his people around and entered the sprawling structure from the rear. Corporal Anthony's squad, on point, rushed the mansion's front door with Kane's squad following them. The door was far too thick and armored to simply kick through. Cody, a member of Anthony's squad, slapped a charge of C4 onto the door.

"Fire in the hole!" Cody shouted and everyone took cover. The charge detonated, blowing the door apart.

Corporal Anthony was the first one into the mansion. The lights in its gigantic foyer were out. The beam of the flashlight mounted on his rifle's barrel swept over the room. It appeared to be completely clear.

Other Marines rushed into the room with him, fanning out to truly secure it. Once that was done, Kane, Neil, and Higgs grouped up in its center alongside him.

"This room is clear, sir," Flynn reported to Anthony. "And not a sign of anyone, alive or otherwise."

Anthony nodded at Flynn, sending him away, as Higgs snorted. "What? We were expecting a welcoming party?"

"Stow it, Higgs," Neil cautioned the NCO.

"What's the plan, sir?" Kane asked.

"We know there's supposed be some kind of giant complex under this place. I'd say that's the best place to start. It was likely where everyone was when things went to hell here," Neil said. "Higgs, I want you to keep your squad up here. Go through this mansion and see what you can find. Everyone else, you're with me, at least until we find the entrance to the complex."

"Brin!" Neil barked.

The geeky little specialist came running over. "Sir?"

"Have you been able to locate the entrance to the complex below yet?" Neil asked.

Brin was holding some sort of high tech, scanner contraption. He held it up, moving the thing around slowly, frowning. "I'm not 100% on it, sir, but I think I've got a general idea."

Neil cocked an eyebrow at the specialist. "I am gonna need more than that from Brin when we get in there. There were no layouts of this place that even the higher up brass could get their hands on."

"At least not that they were willing to show us," Higgs grumbled under his breath.

Ignoring the NCO, Neil said. "Regardless, you're our eyes and ears, Brin. Without you, we'll be blind down there. You understand me?"

"Copy that, Sergeant," Brin nodded fiercely, "I'll

do my best."

"Well then, kid, what are you waiting for?" Kane snapped. "Lead the way!"

"Yes sir!" Brin stood up straighter and got moving. Two other members of Kane's squad moved with him in a formation that at least gave them a good chance of protecting the geeky specialist.

Brin led them to a doorway that was partially open. Beyond it was what would have been a normal office style room except for the fact that it had a wall which was halfway slid sideways, opening into another apparently hidden room. The specialist stopped, falling back so the other Marines with him could deal with any danger that might be waiting on them. Bueler kicked the door. It swung inward revealing a better look at the fragging, crazy room behind it. The "secret" room looked like something from a Star Trek set. There were computers and monitor screens everywhere. There was only one workstation within the room. A man was sprawled out onto it.

Lee was shoved aside by Bueler as the medic went to examine the civilian at the console. He didn't bother to check for a pulse after rolling him over. The man was clearly dead. His face was a bloody mess. Most of it had been slashed away. It looked as if something with razor sharp claws had struck with enough force to break his neck at the same time.

"Frag me," Bueler gasped, crossing himself at the

sight of the dead man's savaged face.

"What the hell did that?" Brin blurted out.

"No fragging idea," Lee answered. "Nothing human, that's for sure. Those weren't made by any kind of blade. You can tell claws did that just from the pattern and how the meat of his face was spread."

"Forget about him," Neil barked, entering the room himself. "He's dead. There's nothing we can do for him. Brin, where's that fragging entrance?"

"Right over there, sir," Brin pointed at the room's far wall.

Everyone's attention shifted to the metal door there.

"Ain't no charge taking that thing down," Cody shook his head, stepping into the room behind Neil.

"Don't need one," Brin managed a weak grin. "I can open it. Just give me a second to get my gear synched up with the controls here."

Neil wished that Higgs was going with them when Brin got the door open but knew that he needed the NCO to hang back, not just to check out the mansion itself but as backup if the crap really hit the fan down there in the complex they were heading for.

"What's taking so long?" Corporal Anthony asked Brin.

"This whole place has gone into some sort of lockdown. Someone either really didn't want whatever is behind that door getting out or anyone getting in," Brin shrugged and returned his attention to whatever the heck he was doing with the tablet/sensor thing in his hand.

"Got it!" Brin said, stepping back from the console he'd been working at as the huge metal door on the far wall slid open.

Several of the Marines in the room had their weapons aimed at it. Nothing came charging out of it but a horrid smell washed over them all. It was like the stench of rotting flesh, sulfur, salt, and a tinge of something that was tangy and unidentifiable. . . at least to Neil.

"I've been able to access the entire system as I hoped, sir," Brin mumbled through the hand covering his nose and mouth. "I should be able to control things in the complex below from here and I've downloaded a map of it as well."

Neil had to admit he was impressed. "Good job, kid. I'm gonna need you to stay up here with Higgs and his squad then.

"Higgs, I'm going to need your boys to stay here with Brin. I need someone to make sure he stays safe and this room isn't compromised," Neil ordered.

"Roger that, sir," Higgs said without arguing though it was clear the NCO didn't want to give up any of his squad for a babysitting gig like this.

"This place is messed up," Brin commented.

"No kidding," Higgs quipped.

Neil moved to stand beside Brin at the work station, looking over the specialist's shoulder at the map of the Drake Complex Brin had pulled up on it.

"What are those?" Neil asked, pointing at one of the larger areas that appeared be to separated from the rest of the complex.

"According to the data, those are all containment cells. There are thirteen of them in total," Brin answered. "Several of them have been breached. That's why they're flashing red whereas the others show as green."

"Breached?" Neil eyed Brin.

"Well, they all seem to be containment cells, sir. Each has its own controlled environment for whatever it's holding. The ones that are lit up in red . . . whatever was in them is out now," Brin explained.

"Does that mean you can tell me what we're up against then?" Neil pressed the specialist.

Brin shook his head. "The cells are only listed as numbers, sir. Sorry."

"Copy that," Neil sighed, his hope of getting easy answers to what had gone down on the island crushed. "But is there anything you can tell me that might help keep us alive or find any survivors that are left here?"

"Uh. . .be careful," Brin stammered, not really having a better answer to the Sergeant's question. "I'll keep digging in the system and see what other information I can find on what's in the cells or was in them as the case may be. The only other thing I can tell you right now is that there's movement all over the place down there in the complex. Could be surviviors or. . ."

Neil put a hand on Brin's shoulder, stopping him. "Just keep at it," Neil ordered. "And let me know as soon as you find anything else that might be helpful."

"Will do," Brin promised.

Two Marines, one of them squad leader Kane, had moved on through the doorway, checking out what lay beyond it.

"We got more bodies in here!" Neil heard Kane shout.

Neil walked through the door. The room was lit by flickering, red emergency lights. Under their harsh glow, he could see the bodies of two men and a woman. One of the men wore a uniform similar to their combat fatigues. He could only be a security officer. Being armed and geared up hadn't done squat in terms of saving his life. His right arm was missing, sheared clean off, leaving the bloody white bone of his shoulder joint exposed. The security officer's expression was that of sheer terror, mouth and eyes opened wide, locked that way forever in death. The other man, or rather what was left of him, had been ripped in two. His entire lower half was gone like the security officer's arm. But it was the poor woman that made Neil sick to his stomach. Something had gutted her from her groin up to just below the bottom of her ribcage. Whatever had done it hadn't stopped there either. Where the woman's breasts had once been were cavities of savaged and torn flesh. Dried spit, blood, and vomit smeared her lips and cheeks. She'd been alive when the mutilations started from the look of things. Neil hoped the woman had let go of life before the worst parts of what had been done to her. As used to death as he was, Neil turned his head away from her corpse. He couldn't take looking at it anymore.

"These folks were hit hard and fast, sir," Kane told him.

"Yeah, but by what?" Corporal Anthony asked, walking up to stand next to Neil.

"Guess we'll find out soon enough," Neil said and motioned at the elevator.

****

Corporal Anthony's squad was the first to ride the lift down into the depths of the Drake Complex. Once Anthony reported that the area was clear, Kane's squad went next followed by Neil's own. The area the lift opened into was akin to a giant metal cavern, wide open space, with a series of sealed doorways along its far wall.

When Sergeant Neil stepped out of the lift, some of the Marines were on their knees vomiting, the rest, jumpy and wide alert, had their weapons raised and ready. Suddenly he knew where the smell they'd encountered above came from. It was a thousand times worse here. The floor was slicked with blood and there were scattered corpses mingled with bits and pieces of others everywhere.

"Kane?" Sergeant Neil asked.

"You got me, sir," the squad leader shrugged. "I've never seen anything like this. If you take a closer look at some of. . . the bodies, sir, you can see that something has been gnawing on most of them. And this. . . this was a massacre."

"He ain't kidding," Corporal Anthony said. "There are armed security people amid this carnage. The ones I was able to check so far have weapons that were clearly discharged. These people here. . . they put up a fight."

Kane nodded. "Seems like they got trapped here waiting on the lift to come down and whatever was after them. . ."

"That makes sense," Anthony agreed. "The lift would've been locked down and wouldn't have responded to anything they tried to do."

"Frag," Neil shook his head in disgust and frustration.

"Where do go from here?" Kane asked.

One of the doors on the far side of the area they were in had been forced open. It was likely where whatever had torn apart all the poor people had come at them from. Cody was busy examining it as Lee and Flynn covered him. Bueler stood close by. The medic's face was a stark pale and he still looked to be ttrying to deal with the sight of the mangled corpses that were everywhere.

Neil approached Bueler to check on him.

The medic saw him and didn't even give the Sergeant time to ask before saying, "I'm fine, sir. This is just a lot to take in."

"I'm sure you've seen worse," Neil tried to comfort Bueler.

"Not like this, sir," Bueler frowned. "These people weren't just killed, many of them were partially eaten, maybe even while they were still alive."

Bueler had just confirmed what Kane said about the corpses.

"Any idea of what could have done this?" Neil pressed the medic.

Bueler sighed and shook his head. "Not really. What I can tell you is that more than one creature did all this. You can tell from the variation in the claw and teeth marks on the bodies. And whatever they were, they were strong as hell."

"You got that right," Cody spoke up, agreeing with Bueler. "Take a look at this."

Neil and the medic moved to take a look at what Cody was trying to show them. On the door that had been broken through, there were not only claws marks scratched into its metal but there were fragging hand prints too. Neil stared at one of them in utter disbelief. The print was the size and shape of a grown man's though there was something slightly off about it that he couldn't put his finger on.

"No human being has the strength to do something like this," Cody commented. "What the hell are we up against here, sir?"

Neil didn't answer. Instead, he tapped his comm. "Brin, the doors out of here, can you tell us where they lead to?"

"Most of those lead to individual containment cells, sir," Brin ordered. "There are only two that don't. One of those will take you to the engineering section while the other leads into the rest of the complex where there looks to be quarters for onsite staff, a small mess, a medical bay, some labs, etc. Note, all the corridors that lead to cells can also be accessed from other points within the primary complex."

"Copy that, Brin," Neil responded. "Those are the two doors I want opened then. You can do that, right?"

"Yes sir," Brin confirmed. "Doing so now."

Neil watched as the two doors he had requested opened. Nothing came charging out of either of them. He breathed a sigh of relief at that.

"Here's the plan," Neil's voice was loud and commanding. "Kane, Anthony, I want you two to take your squads down the corridor that leads into the larger part of the complex. Spread out and find what you can find. If something moves and it's not human, fragging blow it to hell. And I want you to stay in constant comm. contact with Brin and myself. That's an order."

Kane and Anthony nodded. Their squads regrouped and moved out together.

Neil's personal squad consisted of himself, Mitchell, and Rigdon. Their fourth man had been Brin who'd needed to be left behind.

Gesturing at the second door Brin had opened, Neil barked, "Mitchell, take point. Let's get moving. God only knows what's waiting for us through there."

****

Higgs was still upset about losing Flanigan to babysitting duty. He'd sent him to watch over Brin inside the mansion's first floor control room. That left only him, Harmse, and Mercer to cover searching the entire fragging surface of the island. They'd started with the mansion but found nothing and no one within it. The place had been cleared out as if someone had evac-ed it. After checking in with Brin and Harrison again, Higgs had led the others outside.

The island was a small one but it was still a lot to cover with just three Marines. Aside from the Drake mansion there were a few dozen houses clustered in a community area to the west. Higgs figured it made more sense to start there than just go wandering about the rest of the island blindly at night.

Higgs led the way with Harmse and Mercer following after him as the trio walked along what served as the main street of the small community. There weren't lights on in any of the houses, at least that could be seen from the outside. Sure, the island's power was down and running on some kind of backup emergency system but one would think that someone in one of the houses would have candles burning or something.

All three of them were already drenched from the pouring rain. The wind was hellish, so strong at times that Higgs found it hard to breathe. It wasn't enough yet to cause them real problems but it didn't show any signs of letting up either.

Catching a glimpse of something moving among the houses, Higgs raised a hand, gesturing for Harmse and Mercer to come to a stop. Both of them kept silent, waiting to see what was going on.

Something gave a guttural grunt from somewhere in the shadows ahead of their position. Even squinting in the direction the sound had come from, Higgs still couldn't see anything in the darkness through the pouring rain.

"What the hell was that?" Mercer asked, her voice tense and on edge.

"Nothing human," Harmse said.

Without warning, the thing in the shadows came charging out at them. Even getting a good look at its snarling face, Higgs didn't have a clue what the creature was. The thing's eyes glowed blue through the darkness and haze of the pouring rain. It was human shaped, standing about six feet tall. The thing wore no clothes. Scales covered its body and there were gills on the sides of its neck. Higgs had read some H.P. Lovecraft in his youth before joining the Corps. He remembered the pulp author's creatures called Deep Ones. That was what this horrid thing reminded him of. Only it was a hell of a lot tougher looking than any of the Deep Ones he'd ever seen. The creature was sleek, fast, fierce, and heavily muscled.

Harmes managed to bring his M27 up in time to get off a burst of rounds at the monster. His rifle roared. The bullets struck the creature, bouncing harmlessly off its scales, unable to penetrate them. Their impact wasn't enough to stop the monster from closing on Harmes either. He screamed as the beast plowed into him, taking him over backwards to the ground beneath it. Gleaming claws flashed as the monster took a swipe at Harmse's face. The claws raked over the soft flesh there, cutting deep grooves in it and tearing away his nose. Blood flew, mingling with the puddled rain Harmse was lying in. He thrashed about under the monster, trying to shove it away.

Mercer quickly moved into a firing position so that she could get a clearer shot at the monster without risking hitting Harmes too much. Her M27 barked as Mercer put a trio of rounds into the monster's back. The thing's head whipped up, turning in her direction, burning blue eyes falling upon her, even though her bullets had no more effect than Harmse's had. The monster gave Harmse a quick punch with a balled up fist smashing into his forehead, knocking him unconscious, and then leapt up to come snarling towards Mercer. She backpedaled, trying to escape the thing's fury. In her desperate retreat, Mercer let loose on full auto aiming for the center of the monster's chest. Rounds sparked off the thing's scales but this time there were enough of them striking the monster to throw it off balance and stop its momentum.

"Get out of there!" Higgs yelled at Mercer. The old, hardened NCO always carried a shotgun with him in addition to his standard issue weapon. Discarding his M27, Higgs shrugged the pump action shotgun from where it was strapped to his back into his hand. Working its pump, he chambered a round and rushed to intercept the monster closing in on Mercer. The beast reached Mercer before he could catch it. She brought up her M27, blocking its attack, as the monster lashed out at her. Its claws scraped along the metal of the rifle, actually leaving marks in the metal. Somehow Mercer managed to keep her hold on the weapon though. The monster raised its arm to swing at her again but Higgs stopped it from doing so, his shotgun thundering.

The blast from Higgs' shotgun slammed into the monster's side. The heavy slug tore through the scales there opening up a large wound in a shower of exploding gore and foul black blood. The monster squealed at the pain it had to be in and threw itself away from Mercer, whirling about to make a run for it. Higgs wasn't going to let the fragging thing get away after what it had done to Harmes. He hoped Harmse was still alive but even if he was, the damage the thing inflicted would leave him scarred for the rest of his life. Working his shotgun's pump again, Higgs chambered a fresh round and took a second shot at the monster, catching the fleeing beast in the center of its back. Higgs heard the cracking sound of the heavy slug shattering the monster's spine inside of it. The beast was knocked forward, stumbling, and collapsed onto the muddy ground with a loud splash. Higgs sprinted to where the creature had fallen, getting into position to finish it before the thing could get back onto its feet. His shotgun boomed a third time as he fired point blank into the monster's skull. The monster's head blew apart, bits of bone, black blood, and brain matter bursting outward in every direction. Its headless corpse slumped back into the mud and lay there twitching.

Higgs stood over the monster's corpse still wondering just what in the hell the thing was. The name he could think to call it that made any real sense was "merman". It sounded better than fishman at any rate.

"Frag me," Higgs heard Mercer mutter.

Her brush with being torn apart by the thing had been a close one.

"You okay?" Higgs asked, eying her.

"Fine, sir," Mercer nodded.

"Then get over there and check on Harmse," Higgs ordered.

Mercer hurried to where Harmse lay, dropping down beside him to press two of her fingers to the side of his neck but realized she didn't need to.

"He's still breathing," Mercer told him as Higgs watched her.

"Do what you can for him," Higgs snapped, "But do it quick. I don't like being exposed out here like this. There's no reason to think that thing was out here alone."

"You don't really think there are more of those things, do you?" Mercer asked, getting out her medkit and going to work on patching up Harmse as best she could.

Higgs didn't need to answer her. Mercer's question was answered by the chorus of inhuman, screeching cries that rang out in the night around them. He didn't even ask if Harmse was in any shape to be moved. Higgs stepped over and yanked the Marine up. Harmse gave a pained moan as he was hauled to his feet but didn't fully regain consciousness.

"We gotta get the hell out of here right now," Higgs warned Mercer. Every instinct inside of him told the NCO that they needed to run. As much as it took to kill the single monster they'd fought, he knew trying to make a stand against a pack of the creatures was nothing short of suicide.

Higgs couldn't move fast, no matter how much he wanted to, dragging along a semi-conscious Harmse with him. Mercer matched what speed he was capable of as they moved out. Her eyes darted about, peering through the rain for any sign of other creatures like that one they had just killed. It was anybody's guess how many there were on the island. From what they heard though, it was way too fragging many.

Blood dripped from Harmse's mangled face. Higgs did his best not to look at what was left of it. Harmse was dang lucky to be alive. Higgs could hear air whistling in through what remained of Harmse's nose. The sound was sickening.

"Flanigan!" Higgs shouted over his comm. "We've got hostiles!"

Higgs' comm. crackled, seeming to be cutting in and out.

"Can you repeat that, sir?" Flanigan responded. "I didn't copy."

Higgs stopped moving, Mercer sweeping the barrel of her M27 around in a wide arc, trying to cover him and herself as best she could if they were to be suddenly engaged by the monsters.

"I said we've got hostiles out here, Flanigan,"

Higgs growled. "And we're coming in hot."

There was a moment before Flanigan said anything. "Copy that. I'll meet you at the front of the mansion."

"Negative!" Higgs ordered. "Secure that room where you and Brin are holed up. Fragging well stay there and shoot anything that comes your way and doesn't identify itself."

"Yes sir," Flanigan said.

Minutes passed like hours to Higgs as he dragged Harmse along with him.

Harmse finally came to, mostly anyway. He tried to say something but all that came out of his mangled lips was a horrid gargling noise.

"Can you walk?" Higgs snapped.

Harmse nodded weakly.

Higgs let loose his hold on the wounded Marine after making sure that Harmse really was going to be able to stay on his feet. He'd still slow them down but at least Higgs wouldn't be straining to support him any longer, his hands would be free too. Higgs clutched his shotgun in a white knuckled grip. He kept trying not think about the creatures they were up against. Whatever they were, they weren't human. Hell, they shouldn't even exist in the real world. They were the stuff of B budget horror films and pulp novels come to life. Killing men was something Higgs exceled out. These things. . . they were a hell of a lot tougher.

The trio of Marines reached the gate of the Drake mansion. They were wide open as they had been when their unit first arrived. Higgs fell back to bring up the rear as he motioned for Mercer to help Harmse on through them. He looked back into the distant trees. Within their shadows, Higgs could see over a dozen pairs of glowing blue eyes watching them. Higgs spat on the ground, cursing the monsters. The things seemed to be playing with them like a cat would its food before killing it. With the power off, the gates were too large and heavy for Higgs to close on his own. Glancing over his shoulder, Higgs saw that Mercer had Harmse almost to the mansion's front door.

The Mermen in the distant trees burst forth for them. They came charging across the cleared ground between where they were and Higgs' position at the mansion's gates. Higgs gawked at the creatures for a fraction of a second in shock. He hadn't expected them to make their move yet. They'd caught him utterly off guard. Higgs whirled about and ran to catch up to the others, pushing his body to its limits, legs pumping, breath coming in ragged gasps.

Mercer had shoved Harmse inside the mansion and stood just outside its door, her M27 ready to cover Higgs. The rifle's barrel erupted in a series of flashes as it roared on full auto and Mercer poured fire into the merman chasing after him. Higgs heard the grunts of the one those rounds struck. From the look of sheer terror on Mercer's face as she held down her M27's trigger, Higgs wasn't about to glance around to see how close the monsters were.

Higgs reached the mansion's door and bolted on through it. His booted feet nearly slid out from under him as he skidded to a halt. Mercer's rifle had fallen silent. She was right on his heels and trying to get the door slammed shut. Mercer almost managed it too. She would have if one of the creatures hadn't reached them at the last second. Its hand slipped between the door and its frame, preventing it from being fully closed. Higgs had his shotgun aimed at the door but didn't take a shot at the monster even though Mercer wasn't directly in his line of fire. The merman was too strong for Mercer to force the door the rest of the way shut. With a high pitched screech, the Merman shoved the door back fully open and bounded inside the mansion, coming directly at Higgs. His shotgun boomed, blasting the creature at near point blank range. The heavy slug slammed into the Merman's chest, sending black blood splattering, and threw the merman back out through the open doorway.

Mercer moved to try to close the door again but another merman came rushing inside with two more of its kind following after it.

"Fall back!" Higgs screamed, working the pump of his shotgun to chamber another round.

The three mermen spread out, each going after a

different target, trying to clear the way for even more of the monsters to enter. One of them charged Harmse, who barely seemed to know what was going on. The poor bastard never stood a chance. The merman grabbed hold of him and yanked Harmse's head towards its mouth. There was a disgusting crunching noise as the thing's teeth sunk into his skull.

Mercer was smart enough to already be in a position where she could make a run for it and she did. She had two choices: head for the steps leading upstairs or towards the room where Flanigan was holed up with Brin. Mercer didn't want to lead the creatures to them so she bounded up the stairwell. Two of the Mermen bolted after her.

Higgs saw Mercer run but remained where he was facing down the last of the three Mermen who were already inside the mansion. His shotgun boomed like crashing thunder. The Mermen were apparently a lot more than just the hungry beasts they looked to be. They were learning. This merman started trying to dodge his blast as soon as Higgs had pointed the barrel of his weapon at it. Its efforts resulted in the blast blowing a hole in the frame of the doorway behind it rather than its body. Splinters flew in the air as Higgs cursed, flinging his shotgun onto his shoulder by its strap. That shot had been his last round in the weapon and there was no time to reload it right now. Higgs drew his M18 from the holster on his hip like an Old West gunfighter. The pistol cracked in rapid succession. The merman was brought to an abrupt stop as the shots slammed into it and the creature waved about its arms as if trying to swat the bullets away. Higgs knew just how tough the Merman's scales were and shifted his aim. His next shot pulped one of the merman's eyes inside its socket. The creature wailed in pain, stumbling backwards, slapping a hand over the empty hole where its eye had been. Higgs fired another shot aiming for its throat, hoping the scales there weren't as dense. They were. Black blood exploded outward as the bullet ripped into the merman. The merman made a pained, choking noise, grasping at its mangled throat, as it toppled to the floor of the mansion. Higgs didn't hang around to make sure the monster died. He could see a hell of a lot more of the mermen outside racing towards the open doorway. The sound of gunfire above him reminded that Mercer had headed upstairs and likely needed his help. He thought about trying to contact Flanigan again, warn him and Brin that the things were inside now, but didn't. If they followed the orders he'd already given them, he hoped they'd be fine, especially since the mermen were engaged with himself and Mercer, who were leading them away. Higgs sprinted up the stairs without looking back.

Mercer had turned left at the top of the stairs towards where she knew the master bedroom was from when she'd first arrived and checked out the place in order to secure it. The two mermen after her were fragging fast. Mercer knew she couldn't outrun them. Their snarls were drawing closer with each breath she sucked in as she ran. Knowing there was no other choice, Mercer whirled about, her M27 blazing away on full auto. She swept her rifle back and forth, hosing the two mermen with a barrage of rounds. One of the mermen was caught by them at just the right angle that the creature thrashed sideways, crashing through the second floor banister. The thing squealed in surprise and rage as it toppled through the air. She heard a loud thud as its body struck the first floor below. The other merman became even more enraged than it already was, springing towards her like a streak of lightning. Lashing out, one of its hands batted Mercer's M27 from her hands, breaking her trigger finger in the process. Mercer gritted her teeth, ignoring the sudden pain, and ducked as the creature's other hand took a swipe at her head. Her training kicked in as Mercer kicked the merman in its stomach. The merman was flung backwards, collapsing onto the floor. Mercer assumed a defensive stance, waiting for the thing to jump up and come at her again.

"Get down!" Mercer heard Higgs shout at her in warning. She looked past where the merman was lying to see that the NCO had come up the stairs and was heading her way as he slapped a fresh magazine into his M18. Mercer saw there was a room to her right and dived through its doorway as the merman sprang at her and Higgs opened fire on it. His first two shots sparked harmlessly off the armor-like scales that covered the merman's body but they got its attention. As the merman turned towards Higgs, he popped off another two quick shots aiming for the creature's eyes. That had worked for him before and he was counting on it doing so again. His first shot missed its target, grazing the side of the merman's skull and pinging away. His second shot didn't, snapping the merman's head backwards atop its neck. The merman dropped to the floor with Higgs' bullet buried deep inside its brain.

Darting in the room he'd seen Mercer dive into, Higgs slammed its door shut behind him. He knew it didn't stand a chance in hell of actually keeping the mermen out but it might buy them some time.

"Thanks," Mercer said with a wry grin. "You saved my butt out there."

"We ain't even close to being out of the woods yet, kid," Higgs shrugged.

"Don't suppose you have a plan?" Mercer asked.

Higgs looked around the room for anything that might help them. Around them the walls were lined with bookshelves. A lone deck with a laptop on it sat towards the rear of the room. The only other way out was a window but there were fragging metal security bars over it. Holstering his M18 pistol, Higgs slung his shotgun from where it hung on his shoulder into his hands and went to work reloading it.

"Make an epic last stand?" Higgs suggested.

"That doesn't sound like much of a plan," Mercer commented.

"Well, you come up with a better one, you let me know," Higgs snorted.

From the sounds coming from the other side of the room's door, more of the mermen were closing fast.

"Steady," Higgs cautioned. "No point in wasting rounds trying to shoot through the door. They're going to come through it soon enough."

Outside the room, a merman screeched. A fraction of a second later, a scaled fist pierced the wood of the door sending splinters flying. Higgs and Mercer were far enough back to not be struck by them. A rain of equally heavy blows hammered the door, shattering entire sections of it before scaled hands shoved what was left inward.

As the first merman entered, Higgs met the creature with a blast from his shotgun that reduced its face into a mass of splattering gore. The merman fell flat onto the floor, lying there twitching. Higgs stepped aside, working the pump of his shotgun to give Mercer a clearer line of fire at the doorway. Her M27 let loose a stream of rounds that slammed into the next two of the creatures. Some of them pinged harmlessly away from their scales but a few managed to penetrate them. One merman squealed as a bullet pierced its groin. The other staggered sideways as Mercer's rounds tore at its body. Mercer held her trigger tight until the magazine of her M27 clicked empty. The merman with the groin wound slumped against the wall of the room, unintentionally pulling a bookcase down on top of it and didn't get up. The other merman that had entered with it was leaking putrid black blood from multiple wounds but was fighting to stay on its feet. Two more of the mermen had come in behind those two. Their dark lips were parted in snarls that showed the rows of razor sharp, gleaming teeth inside their mouths.

Mercer retreated as Higgs moved forward again, covering her while she reloaded. A blast from his shotgun blew a gaping hole in the chest of the closest merman. It gave a high-pitched squeal that was cut short as its ribs were torn apart. The creature's corpse collapsed into the path of the other merman coming at Higgs, tripping it up, which gave him time to ready another round. Higgs squeezed the shotgun's trigger as the merman recovered, sprinting at him. Its hand managed to slap the barrel of his shotgun down at the last instant. Instead of delivering the killing shot Higgs had hoped for, the blast instead struck the merman in the upper hip of its right leg. The heavy slug nearly severed the merman's leg entirely from its body. Squealing, the merman lost its balance, toppling over in front of Higgs. Unfortunately, it was still within reach of him. Higgs tried to jump back away from the creature but it was too fast, swinging a clawed hand in a desperate swipe. The merman's claws sunk into Higgs' left leg, tearing their way into his flesh. Higgs screamed, striking at the merman's head with the butt of his shotgun. He brought it downward with all the strength he could muster, smashing it into the top of the merman's skull. The blow was enough to stun the merman for a second but didn't really look to have hurt it otherwise. Higgs fought to free himself from the creature's claws that were imbedded in his leg. The pain of doing so was too intense though and he faltered. The merman grabbed his other leg, pulling him off his feet. Higgs crashed onto his back, the impact with the room's floor knocking the breath from his lungs. The merman grabbed him, hand over hand, yanking the NCO closer. With each grab, the thing's claws punctured his body. Mercer stood watching helplessly, unable to shoot the creature without hitting him too. Higgs grunted, gritting his teeth against each eruption of fresh pain that raced through him, knowing that he had to do something or die. Hell, with the wounds the thing had already dealt him, he might bleed out anyway before the fight to hold the room was over. Higgs had lost his hold on his shotgun. His hand reached to draw his M18, wrenching the pistol free of its holster. He brought the weapon up, pressing its barrel against the underside of the snarling merman's chin. He squeezed its trigger in rapid succession. The M18 boomed over and over again. The top of the merman's head exploded upwards as Higgs' bullets ripped through it. The merman died instantly, the full weight of its corpse slumping onto him. Higgs was too weak to shove the creature off. Mercer had been forced into retreat, leaving Higgs to fend for himself as several other mermen engaged her. Higgs was still straining in vain to get out from under the corpse atop him when the scaled hands of another creature took hold of the sides of his head. He heard the sharp crack of his own neck being snapped before Higgs' world went black.

Mercer lived almost a full half minute longer, trying to drive the monsters back with her M27. The weapon betrayed her, clicking empty, unable to stop the mermen from reaching her. Surrounded by the monsters, Mercer died, screaming at the top of her lungs, as scaled hands tore away her arms from her body before razor sharp teeth ripped away chunks of her flesh. Soon, the room was silent except for the sound of the mermen's wetly smacking lips as they fed upon the remains of the two Marines.

****

Brin and Flanigan had watched Mercer, Higgs, and a staggering Harmse try to hold the creatures at the mansion's front door through its security feeds.

Flanigan freaked when he saw the monsters, not

knowing what they were or if they were really.

"What are those things?" Flanigan had rasped in shock.

"Mermen," Brin had answered him calmly, "the real life version."

It had been a hell of a fight to convince Flanigan not to rush out to join the rest of his squad as they'd seen Harmse die. Brin almost was forced to bodycheck him in order to keep Flanigan from leaving the control room. Thankfully, Higgs had ordered them to seal it up before the mermen made it inside the mansion. The room was hidden and protected by thick metal doors behind fake wooden walls that had slid back into place. Even if the mermen did sniff them out somehow, it was unlikely they'd be able to breach the room.

Flanigan sat beside him now as Brin clicked off the feed to the monitor that showed images of Higgs and Mercer's bodies being fed upon by the mermen. They had lost their brutal fight with the creatures.

"Those things are. . . those things are eating them, man," Flanigan looked sick.

"They can't get in here," Brin reminded him. "We're safe."

"It's not about us being safe!" Flanigan suddenly exploded into a mad rage. "Those are our friends! How the hell can you just sit there like that?"

"Calm down," Brin pleaded, worried Flanigan was about to do something stupid.

"We should have been out there with them," Flanigan snapped.

"If we had been, we'd be dead right now too," Brin sighed. "Think about it, Flanigan. Two more guns wouldn't have made any difference in that fight."

"You don't know that," Flanigan whined.

"I do . . .and you do too," Brin said keeping his voice calm and flat. "Besides, everyone else is counting on us, Flangian. All of them."

Flanigan glared at him, anger still burning in his eyes, but said nothing more. Some part of him had to have realized the truth of what had been said.

"Look, I've got to let the Sergeant know about those things," Brin said. "I need you to take a seat so that I know you're okay for me to do that."

Reluctantly, Flanigan set his M27 down and plopped his butt onto the edge of the console Brin was sitting at.

Brin opened a channel to Sergeant Neil. "Sergeant, this is Brin in the surface control room. Do you copy? Over."

The Sergeant, Mitchell, and Rigdon were en route to the engineering section of the Drake Complex. Brin could see the dots of their standard issue tracking units on the monitor screen moving along at a steady pace.

"Report," Sergeant Neil's voice answered gruffly.

"Sir, Higgs' squad has been eliminated by hostiles

they encountered up here," Brin reported. "Those same hostiles have breached the mansion."

There was a brief moment of silence before Neil asked, "The entire squad?"

"Yes sir." Brin could tell that Neil was still attempting to process what he had been told. He knew that the Sergeant and Higgs were close.

"Is your position secure?" Neil asked.

"I believe it is . . .at least for the time being," Brin replied.

"Good," Neil grunted. "Now, what is it that you're not telling me, Brin?"

"The hostiles, sir, they're mermen," Brin said, just putting the craziness right out there and getting it over with.

"Mermen?" Neil sounded as if he didn't know whether to laugh or start tearing into him for being nuts.

"Mermen, sir," Brin confirmed. "I have visual confirmation on that. Flanigan and I were able to watch their engagement with Higgs' squad via the security feeds here. I think they came from one of the thirteen containment cells listed as being inside the complex. Scratch that, of the twelve. The thirteenth cell is actually so large that it's below the complex not inside of it however I do not believe that it's the one the mermen escaped from."

Brin saw the dots that represented the Sergeant and the other two Marines who were with him stop moving.

"Copy all that," Sergeant Neil responded. "Anything else I need to know, Brin?"

"The mermen appear to be resistant to small arms fire. From what we saw, it takes some real firepower or a lucky shot to injure them. And they're fast, sir. Strong too. I recommend extreme caution should you encounter the creatures," Brin said.

"Understood," Sergeant Neil said. "Keep me informed of your situation. Neil, out."

Brin looked over at Flanigan, "That went well I think."

Flanigan just shrugged.

****

Neil noticed that Mitchell and Rigdon were staring at him. He knew the two of them had overheard his conversation with Brin. They were handling it like the professionals they were, keeping their eyes sharp and faces straight despite the fact that the specialist had told them to be wary of mermen coming after them.

"You heard the man, boys," Neil gave them a wry grin. "Looks like we're going monster hunting for real down here."

"He said the, um, mermen came from one of the thirteen cells," Mitchell frowned. "So just what in the hell are in the other twelve?"

"Let's hope we don't find out," Neil said with no

trace of humor in his voice. "Either way though, best we get on with it."

The squad got moving again. The corridor they were passing through was like all the others they'd seen so far. It was somewhat tube shaped in a sense with plain metal walls and the flicker of red emergency backup lights above them.

A series of rapid clanging noises came from somewhere behind them.

"What the hell?" Rigdon had time to blurt out before everything went to hell.

A thing that resembled a human-sized squid was charging towards them. The creature had two thicker primary tentacles that it was using as if they were legs. The rest of its tentacles whipped wildly through the air around the central mass of its body. It moved with impossible speed. The squid thing reached Rigdon before any of them could open fire. Slamming one of its primary tentacles into the wall of the corridor, its tip pierced the metal there, supporting the weight of its body, as the squid creature lashed out with its other. That second tentacle plunged through Rigdon's body like a spear, tip bursting outward through his back in an explosion of blood. Rigdon hadn't even had time to scream before the squid thing murdered him where he stood.

"Frag that thing!" Neil shouted, squeezing the trigger of his M27.

Mitchell's rifle roared to life as well. Two streams

of fully automatic rounds ripped the squid creature's central mass to shreds. The creature's body was nearly as soft as a real squid's based on how it blew apart from the barrage of bullets that hit it.

Neil raced to where Rigdon had collapsed. The squid thing's tentacle had been yanked out of it as the squid thing died. Neil squatted next to Rigdon, looking him over. Part of him had hoped that Rigdon was still alive somehow despite the gaping hole in his chest but he wasn't. There was no way in hell to survive a wound like the one Rigdon had taken.

More clanging from down the corridor, growing louder as it drew closer to their position.

"Sir!" Mitchell yelled in warning, pointing in the direction of the clanging.

Sergeant Neil rose to his feet, staring at the horrors coming at them. The entire corridor seemed to be filled with more creatures like the one they'd just killed. They scampered along the walls and the ceiling, bounding forward, as well as on the actual floor of the corridor. Neil counted dozens of the monsters at a glance. Only God knew how many of the creatures there really were.

A few of the creatures stopped where Rigdon's corpse was sprawled out on the floor of the corridor. A shiver of revulsion washed over Neil as he saw that the creatures were tearing away chunks of Rigdon's flesh and shoving it into the mouths of their central mass.

"Fall back!" Neil ordered, opening up on the approaching swarm of squid creatures. His M27 roared on full auto. Mitchell retreated side by side with him. One squid thing exploded after another as their rounds tore into the mass of creatures. The others paid no attention to their brethren dying around them, not even slowing as they advanced into the barrage of death the two Marines were dishing out.

Neil knew they were about to be overrun and there wasn't a hell of a lot they could do about it. His M27 clicked empty. Cursing, he ejected its spent magazine, slapping a fresh one into the weapon. The pause he was forced to take in order to do so gave the creatures even that much more of an advantage over the two of them. Mitchell's weapon clicked empty just as Neil brought his back into the battle. Blazing away at the monsters, he continued to backpedal.

Mitchell didn't bother to attempt to reload his rifle. Instead, he pulled a grenade from his combat vest, yanking out its pin, and lobbed it into the mass of swarming squid creatures.

"Watch it!" Mitchell shouted.

The grenade landed squarely in the midst of the swarm of creature, detonating there. The blast ripped half a dozen of the monsters to pieces, wounding others. The sigh reminded Neil of when a real squid would spray a cloud of ink into the water around it, the shower of black splattering through the air and wasn't ink but the foul, putrid blood of the squid things. Even the blast didn't give the creatures pause though. Those that had survived it and were still able to move surged forward just as quickly as they been without any regard for what had just happened. The squid things either had to be nearly mindless or so driven by hunger that they were blind to everything else.

Neil and Mitchell reached a bend in the corridor. It curved around to the right. Seeing that the bend was a chance for them to stop trying to hold the things back, even as they slowly retreated, and finally make a full out run for it, Neil glanced over at Mitchell. Neil saw that he must have had the same idea and nodded at him.

As they rounded the bend, both of them stopped firing into the swarming mass of squid creatures and ran like hell. Neil jerked out the only grenade he was carrying and lobbed it behind the two of them in the hope of bettering their odds of escaping the monsters. The grenade blew. Its thunderous blast echoed along the corridor. Neil's legs pumped under him as his lungs felt like they were on fire. He was pushing his body as hard as it could stand and then some. Mitchell vanished from his sight as Neil pulled slightly ahead of him in the corridor. Up ahead, Neil saw that their path was blocked by a sealed, bulkhead door. There was a control pad on the wall to the door's left but he sure as hell didn't have the code to make it work and no time to radio Brin for help either. It was a long shot but Neil raised his M27 putting a round into it as he ran. Sparks flew as the bullet struck the control pad. By the grace of God, it must have shorted things out in just the right way because the bulkhead door opened ahead of him.

Glancing around with a wild grin of relief on his face, Neil looked back, his eyes scanning for Mitchell. His grin was transformed into a grimace as he heard Mitchell screaming. Neil saw that one of the lead squid creatures had managed to whip out a primary tentacle that now ensnared Mitchell's leg. The creature yanked on it, bringing Mitchell down hard and flat against the metal floor of the corridor. There was a sharp crunching noise as Mitchell's nose struck it. Mitchell grunted in pain and then rolled over onto his back as the squid creature dragged him in its direction. Others of the creatures were already coming around it, closing in. Mitchell opened up with his M27 on full auto. He had managed not to lose the weapon in his fall. The M27 roared, spitting spent casings from its side, as Mitchell swept it back and forth, hosing the swarm of squid creatures at point blank range. His bullets tore and ripped at the soft bodies of the squid creatures. They severed limbs and blew apart the central masses of several of the monsters. Black blood flew and splattered all over and around Mitchell. It was a futile effort but Neil could see that Mitchell wasn't going to die without taking as many of the fraggers with him as he could.

Neil knew rationally that there was nothing he could do to save Mitchell. If he stopped to try, he'd die too. There was no question of that. Still, leaving one of his men behind was something he couldn't deal with. Neil skidded to a halt, whipping the barrel of his rifle around at the swarm of squid creatures. He let loose on them, squeezing the trigger of his M27 tight. Neil kept his aim above where Mitchell was fighting for his life on the floor. Three of the squid creatures were on Mitchell now. One of the things had jerked his rifle from his hands and held it high in the air with one of its lesser tentacles as it stabbed at Mitchell with its others. A second squid creature's primary tentacles were wrapped around his arms, trying to press them flat to the floor above Mitchell's head as he struggled against them. The third creature crept up Mitchell's legs, slinking over them, as its mouth approached his groin. Mitchell wailed in terror and pain as the thing's teeth closed on his genitals, biting them off of his body. Then Mitchell couldn't be seen anymore as the swarm of squids pressed on over and passed him, trapping him beneath them.

"Frag it!" Neil blurted out, watching Mitchell disappear under the surging squid creatures. He leaped through the doorway he'd shot open, slapping at the control panel on the side he was on now.

Shockingly, it actually worked. The door slammed down between Neil and the squid creatures, preventing the things from being able to get at him. He could hear the monsters bashing their primary tentacles against the other side of the door even through its thick metal but the door looked stable. The creatures wouldn't be getting through it any time soon.

Neil stood there, sweat dripping from him, catching his breath. Both Mitchell and Rigdon were dead. As the emotions of that fact fully hit him, Neil bashed a balled up fist into the wall of the corridor in anger. Doing so hurt like hell. He forced himself to get a grip on things and regain his focus.

He heard something squeal behind him. Turning, Neil saw something that looked like a deformed ape with the lower body of a fish crawling along the corridor towards him. The razor-like teeth inside its snarling mouth gleamed in the red emergency lights. The thing's body was insanely out of proportion. Its arms were massive muscled things that ended in giant-sized hands. There were sprouts of brownish-red hair that grew amid the scales that covered the bulk of its body. Its skin or scales, whatever you wanted to call it, over the monkey thing's face was so taut that it was like looking at a skeleton. There was rage in its glowing, yellow eyes as the thing heaved itself at him. One of its hands closed on the barrel of his rifle, crushing and bending it, rendering the weapon useless. Neil jumped away, trying to get out of the monster's reach, only to slam his back into the metal of the door that was behind him. There was nowhere to escape to. His right hand drew his sidearm, yanking the pistol free of its holster. He fired the pistol directly into the ape monster's face. Bright red blood splashed onto him as the bullets buried themselves in the monster's forehead. The beast shook its head, slinging more blood everywhere but refused to die. Its other hand grabbed hold of Neil's left arm, breaking it. Before Neil could recover, the ape fish thing rose up from the floor, climbing onto his body, its weight pulling him down some in the process. Its gleaming teeth found the soft flesh of his neck and bit into him there. Neil instinctively wrenched his head back from the thing, tearing away most of his throat. The ape fish monster slapped at him, knocking his spasming form the rest of the way to the floor. Neil was already dead as the freakish creature began to eat him.

****

"Damn!" Brin's knuckles were white from where he was clenching his hands tight. Again, he and Flanigan had watched helplessly as more of their unit died. Somehow this time was worse because it had been the Sergeant and his squad. Sergeant Neil was the toughest person Brin had ever known. If even that bastard couldn't stay alive down there in the hell hole of a monster pit this island was, what hope did the two of them have?

Brin hadn't been able to reach Sergeant Neil and his squad during their encounter with the squid creatures. He didn't know if it was because of how close the Sergeant and his squad had been to the complex's engineering section or if the squid creatures themselves were to blame, maybe generating some sort of limited bio-electromagnetic pulse around them. Brin doubted if it really would have mattered if he had been able to reach them during those last moments before they were all torn apart but the guilt that weighed on him was heavy nonetheless.

Flanigan looked sick. His skin was pale and his forehead spotted with beads of sweat. Brin couldn't blame him. It was as if they had somehow left the real world behind the moment they had set foot on the island because the monsters that were killing their unit were insane. They were things that shouldn't exist, things straight out of some sicko's darkest and most perverted nightmares. Frag, that thing that took out the Sergeant was messed up. What in the hell was it? Some kind of monkey fish? Frag. Brin shook his head to try to clear it of that sickening image.

"What the frag are we going to do, man?" Flanigan muttered. "The Sergeant is dead. That thing is eating him right now while we're sitting here."

Brin shrugged. "Things are pretty fragging bad. .
.I'll give you that but we're still safe in here and both
Kane and Corporal Anthony's squads are still out
there."

"You should get them the hell out and call for us
an evac," Flanigan grumbled. "We're not trained to
go up against. . . whatever the frag these things are
on this island."

"We can't do that, Flanigan," Brin argued. "Our
job here isn't done yet."

"What fragging job?" Flanigan raged. "There
ain't nobody here left to save! Have you seen a
single living soul since we got here, Brin? Have
you?"

"We have to keep looking," Brin frowned. "And
you know we do. There could be people down there
that need us."

"Yeah well, how many of us have to die just to
make sure the rich bastards aren't all dead already?"
Flanigan glared at Brin.

"Flanigan. . ." Brin tried to find words that would
get him to settle down. "We can't give up yet.
Besides, with that storm out there, even if I did call
for evac it would likely be hours coming."

"You should call them back, Brin," Flanigan
pressed him again.

"Technically, Corporal Anthony is the
commanding officer now," Brin said. "So even if I

wanted to, it's his call not mine."

"Then get him on the line and tell him what the hell is going on already," Flanigan looked ready to go berserk on him if he didn't.

Brin nodded, opening a channel to Corporal Anthony's squad. "Beta squad, this is Specialist Brin, over."

"What the frag do you want, Brin?" the Corporal's voice growled at him in response. "We just had a run in with a bloody sea snake! It took out Flynn."

Neither Brin or Flanigan said anything though they exchanged a concerned look.

"We've got the bastard thing locked out of the section we're currently in but you need to let Sergeant Neil and the others know that there really are fragging monsters down here," Corporal Anthony ordered Brin.

"I can't do that, sir," Brin sighed over the comm. "Sergeant Neil and his squad are dead."

"Frag," Corporal Anthony spat. "More sea snakes?"

"Uh. . . no sir," Brin said. "They were taken out by what looked to be amphibious squid creatures."

"And you're just now reporting this?" the Corporal sounded ticked off at being kept out of the loop.

"It gets worse, sir," Brin went on, "Higgs and his squad on the surface have been wiped out as well. They were eaten by things that appeared to be mermen."

"You've got to be kidding me," Corporal Anthony's voice was tense and filled with frustration.

"Wish I was, sir," Brin responded. "We were able to watch both Sergeant Neil and Higgs' squad being taken out. It wasn't pleasant. Flanigan is eager for you to give the word and have me call in evac copters for the rest of us."

"Negative on that crap," Corporal Anthony snapped. "You tell Flanigan to get himself together and man up."

"Copy that," Brin nodded.

Flanigan had heard the Corporal's reply and sat next to Brin, scowling, though he did keep his mouth shut.

"What's your status, Brin?" Corporal Anthony asked.

"Our position is secure at least for the time being, sir," Brin assured him. "We don't have eyes on you though. There's something in that section of the complex that's scrambling the feeds from the cameras there."

"And Kane's squad? Do you have eyes on them?" the Corporal pressed him.

"Yes sir," Brin said. "They're moving slowly through the complex, parallel to where you seem to be."

"Get in touch with them and let them know what's going on," Corporal Anthony ordered. "They need to know what they're up against down here and we can't afford to lose anyone else."

"What about you, sir?" Brin asked.

"We're going to keep moving down here, see what we can find without getting eaten," Corporal Anthony grunted. "Let me know when you're able to get eyes on us. God knows we could use some help navigating this fragging place. Anthony, out."

"No call for evac," Brin reminded Flanigan before he could say anything more. "You heard the Corporal."

Flanigan nodded, sullen and defeated. . . but then Flanigan perked up and not in a good way. Something had caught his eye on the monitor that was showing Kane and his squad. "What in the fragging hell is that?"

Brin looked at the screen Flanigan was pointing at, his jaw dropping open in utter shock.

****

Squad leader Kane, Bueler, Lee, and Urban kept a steady but cautious pace as they moved through the web of interlocking corridors of the Drake Complex. Urban was on point with Lee bringing up the rear. Kane was in the middle with Bueler. He knew Bueler could take care of himself but Kane still liked having the medic close where he could keep an eye on him. If things hit the fan, Bueler's skill set might be the only thing that kept them alive in the aftermath.

Brin's voice suddenly came over the comm. in Kane's helmet.

"Gamma squad, come in. Over," the specialist called out.

"Kane here," he answered.

"Be advised the complex is crawling with hostiles," Brin told him. "Our unit has taken heavy losses, two squads wiped out entirely so far."

"Frag me," Kane muttered in disbelief. "Which two?"

"The squad on the surface and Sergeant Neil's too," Brin reported.

"The old man is dead?" Kane shook his head, not wanting to believe what he was hearing.

"Afraid so," Brin confirmed. "Corporal Anthony has assumed command. His squad is moving through the complex on a course parallel to yours though I haven't been able to get an exact reading on their location."

Kane could feel the eyes of his squad mates on him. They were all hearing what he was over the open channel Brin was using. Urban looked ready to go on a rampage while Bueler and Lee wore expressions of extreme concern.

"Copy that," Kane nodded. "What can you tell us about these hostiles?"

"They're greatly varied in their nature and methods but none of them are human," Brin sounded completely serious despite what he'd just said.

"Come again," Kane blinked. "What do you mean not human?"

"I've had visual confirmation on three types of . . . uh. . . monsters, sir," Brin said. "We've got what appear to be mermen on the surface. The closest to your position that I know of though are some type of air breathing squids that use their primary tentacles as if they were legs. Be warned, those things are fast and strong as hell."

Lee's expression of concern had become a wry smirk. Urban's hadn't changed. The man still just looked like he needed something in front of him that he could blow to Hell. Bueler had gone pale, his eyes bugging in their sockets.

"Are you yanking my chain, Brin?" Kane demanded. "If you are, I'll see to it that the Sergeant has you up on charges the second we're back aboard the ship."

"Negative, sir," Brin said. "Sergeant Neil is dead. As I said, Corporal Anthony is in command now."

"That guy's lost it," Lee chuckled. "Must have lost it from the stress of trying to run things from up there."

It was Flanigan's voice that came over the comm. next. "Nerd boy isn't making any of this up, Kane. I saw it all too. You guys better watch your butts down there or you'll get them chewed off."

"Roger that," Kane responded, beginning to accept just what an insane mess they were in. "We'll stay frosty and sharp. What are the Corporal's orders?"

"Anthony hasn't changed your existing ones. Work your way through the complex, render aid to any survivors you encounter, bringing them with you, and meet up with his squad at the predetermined rally point," Brin, apparently not having anything else to pass on to them ended the transmission.

"We don't get paid enough for this kind of crap," Urban snarled, working on the pump on his combat shotgun to chamber a round.

"Monsters, huh?" Lee shrugged. "And here I was thinking I'd seen everything after our stint in the Sand Box."

Bueler remained silent, his expression fearful and grim.

"Shut up and keep moving," Kane ordered, getting his own head back in the game.

Lee took over point from Urban who moved to take a turn watching the rear of the squad.

"You smell that?" Bueler asked as they walked along the corridor they were in. "It's like somebody drenched everything ahead of us in vinegar or something."

Bueler wasn't wrong. The stench was so pungent it made Kane cringe and wiggle his nose.

"What the hell is that?" Lee asked no one in particular.

"Look!" Bueler blurted out, pointing at the ceiling

several yards beyond their position. A large section of it appeared to have been burnt away. They could see into the level of the complex above them through it.

"No, man," Lee said. "Look at that!"

Beneath the hole in the corridor's ceiling there was something lying on its floor. Whatever the thing was, it was almost invisible. If Lee hadn't spotted it, Kane wasn't sure he would have noticed the thing at all until he'd been right on top of it. Whatever it was, it was almost completely transparent. As Kane stared at the amorphous pile of goo, there really was no other way to describe the thing, it seemed to be just barely moving as if it were breathing.

Bueler walked past Lee, leaving his place at Kane's side.

"Man, I wouldn't. . ." Lee stammered.

"Bueler," Kane called the medic's name in warning.

The medic was very cautiously approaching the mass of. . .whatever the hell it was.

"It's okay," Bueler said. "I just want to check this thing out. I'm pretty sure it can't move."

Kane wasn't buying that assumption after everything Brin had just told them.

"Get back here right now, Bueler," Kane barked. "That's an order."

"But sir. . ." Bueler started, turning around to face him. The medic never got to finish his sentence.

The oozing, transparent glob rose up from the floor and hurled itself over him, enveloping Bueler within it. Kane could see the medic's mouth open in a scream that was silenced by the crap covering him.

Urban's shotgun swung up level with Bueler and the glob, but Kane rushed to shove its barrel downward.

"Hold your fire, man," Kane ordered.

All of them watched in horror as Bueler's combat suit was cooked off of him. His skin bubbled, melting away from his bones. Droplets of red boiled inside the creature's mass. Kane was sure that the thing was alive somehow now and out to get them.

Within seconds, there was nothing left of Bueler except his bones and the parts of his gear that were made of metal. The amorphous goo thing oozed off of what was left of the medic towards the rest of them. If it hadn't, Kane figured even Bueler's bones would have been dissolved too. If the hole in the ceiling was any indication, the acid inside the thing was strong enough to eat through almost any fragging thing that it touched.

"That thing ate Bueler!" Lee yelled.

"Frag it!" Urban barked, opening fire despite Kane's earlier order.

Urban's shotgun thundered. The heavy slug that the weapon spat splashed into the blob sending some of its goo splattering into the air. If the blob thing felt the slug's impact, it gave no indication of it. The blob splashed forward across the floor of the corridor at Lee. Startled and utterly freaked out, Lee let loose at the thing with his rifle on full auto. The rounds he fired all hit the nearly transparent glob entering its mass. Most of them exited its other side but a few were eaten away to nothingness before they could. Lee screamed as the creature reached him. It rose up like a towering tidal wave above him and then came crashing down. Lee's flesh was melted away as the thing consumed most of his body, leaving only his bones floating around inside of it.

"Sir!" Urban yelled at Kane.

Bullets didn't damage the amorphous creature in the slightest. They either just passed through its body or were consumed by the acids within it. The more powerful rounds from Urban's shotgun had blown chunks of it away from the thing's central mass, sure, but even that hadn't really done anything that clearly caused it pain or even slowed it down. They had to come up with a means of stopping the creature. . .and fast too.

"Get the Hell out of there!" Kane barked.

Urban fell back, retreating from the amorphous creature. Kane stood, motioning him on towards the doorway down the corridor from their current position. As soon as Urban had cleared the doorway, Kane darted through after him, and smashed a fist into the controls on the wall next to it. Sparks flew but his blow had the desired effect. The bulkhead door violently slammed into place.

"That won't hold it," Urban warned.

"I know," Kane nodded, "but it'll buy us time."

"Time? What for?" Urban asked.

"To figure out how to kill it," Kane growled.

"God have mercy!" Urban pointed at the bulkhead door. Its metal was bubbling. . .popping and crackling. "It's already coming through!"

"Toss me your grenade!" Kane ordered.

Urban removed it from the pouch on his belt and threw it over.

Kane caught the grenade, his own already out, and dropped to one knee so that he could shrug off his backpack and rummage around inside of it, searching for the roll of duct tape he knew was in it. Kane hurried, taping the two grenades together.

"You really think that's going to work?" Urban changed out the magazine of his automatic shotgun for a fresh one.

"If you've got a better plan," Kane grunted, "I'm all ears."

What solid parts of the thick bulkhead door remained gave way, steaming metal splashing onto the floor of the corridor as the nearly transparent creature oozed through.

Kane yanked the pins from the taped together grenades, throwing them into the monster's mostly liquid form. The grenades exploded, blowing the creature completely apart, splashing globs of its form everywhere. Urban had already fallen back but even where he had withdrawn to, bits of the creature hit him. Kane was covered by the creature's goo. He screamed, howling in pain, as the globs that landed on him burnt completely through the parts of his body they made contact with. Droplets bubbled where they landed on his cheeks and hands. Kane watched in horror as those droplets opened up holes in his hands as if he had been crucified. Other drops melted through the flesh of his cheeks onto his teeth, and then through them deep into the bones of his face. Kane collapsed onto the floor, dead, and smoldering.

Urban was yelling and cursing. A larger glob of the creature had splashed over his lower right leg. His clothes and flesh there were gone. He could see the entirety of his leg bone between his knee and ankle. And that sight was the last he saw as his mind shut down from the shock of the pain and trauma as the world went black before his eyes.

****

Reggie was curled up beneath the desk that filled the center of the office he was hiding in. It was deep in the lower levels of the Drake Complex. The office had belonged to Director Smith but he was dead now like everyone else as far as Reggie knew. Most of the monsters held in the Drake Complex were free. The Charon had freed the Mermen first and things had just gone to hell from there. Between the fish guys rampaging throughout the place and power outages caused by the Charon eating its way through the complex's walls, very few of Mr. Drake's precious creatures were still contained.

In the last hours of his life, Reggie had seen more horrors than he would have thought possible. The Mermen had ripped apart Powell with their bare hands and gobbled up his flesh and fat as if they were starving children and he'd been made of candy. The Charon had caught up with Rachel and himself as they fled the massacre Mr. Drake's party had become. The creature had rushed them from behind, knocking Rachel from her feet, consuming the lower half of her body as he'd tried to pull her through the airlock that had been closing between them and the creature. Reggie would never forget the smell of her bubbling intestines as the strands of them being pulled and stretched between the part of her inside the creature and the rest of her body snapped. He'd never forget the sight of it either. Just the thought of it made Reggie feel like he was about to throw up. The two of them had barely escaped the rest of the monsters running amok only for her to end up. . . Reggie shook his head, forcing the memories of Rachel's death away.

Reggie had always thought of Drake as a full of himself prick but even so hadn't really believed things could ever get so out of control. Sure, holding all the monsters here was a dangerous thing. That hadn't meant it couldn't be done though. Reggie and the others had taken every possible precaution and most of the security and science staff had taken their jobs with a deadly seriousness. Reggie was forced to admit to himself that he was just as in shock as Drake was when the claws of a merman's scaled hand disemboweled him.

Having utterly lost track of the passage of time, Reggie couldn't say how long he'd been hiding in the office. He knew that staying where he was, was just asking for one of the complex's monsters to stumble onto him eventually. They'd be prowling the complex and the island in search of prey. He needed to get moving, find a way out of the complex and get the hell off the island. There was a rumor among the security personnel that Director Smith had called in favors, using Drake's name, to have a Navy warship stationed nearby tonight. It was a wise precaution to take. The guy might be a jerk but he wasn't always an idiot. Likely, Smith had been mostly concerned with the safety of the rich and powerful guests that Drake had invited, their safety being of the upmost importance, but if that ship really was out there, then his own chances of survival improved greatly. The C.O. of the ship would have almost certainly dispatched a rescue team to the island by now. All he had to do was find a means of making contact with them.

The complex's internal phone system was down and its intercoms spotty at best. His best option was to get moving, head for the surface, and assess his situation again from there if he didn't run into help by then. While Reggie didn't truly know how much time had passed, he felt confident that if help was coming, at least in time to matter, it was already on the island somewhere.

Reggie crawled out from underneath the desk. His legs were sore and didn't want to move properly. He set his pistol within easy reach and rubbed at them, getting the blood there flowing again faster. It was eerily quiet both inside the office and in the corridor outside of it. That was a good sign. . . or he hoped it was. Poking his head up over the top of the desk, Reggie looked around the office and the thick plexiglass of its door. There was no sign of any danger close by. Using the edge of the desk, Reggie hauled himself up onto his feet after grabbing his pistol. He desperately wished for a more powerful weapon. The pistol, while far better than nothing, wasn't much when you were up against monsters like mermen, sea snakes, or worse. It wouldn't do squat against the Charon. If he ran into that thing and couldn't get away, Reggie knew that would be the end of him.

He and Rachel had fled deeper into the complex while the party goers were being massacred. Reggie told himself that there was nothing they could have done to help them. If he didn't, thinking about the guilt would break him. He and Rachel had lacked the firepower to do anything that wouldn't have simply gotten them killed too in the process so they had run. The problem was, Reggie realized now, it had been in the wrong direction. Rachel wanted to head for a nearby weapons cache but they weren't able to make it there. . . Regardless, he'd ended up in this office. What he needed to do wasn't head deeper into the complex, weapons cache close by or not. His plan was to head back out of the complex and try to reach the surface without getting killed by the monsters wandering around down here in search of prey.

Reggie slipped out of the office and took a moment to get his bearings while keeping an eye out for anything inhuman lurking in the shadows. The power was out in this section of the complex. The area was lit only by the flickering, dim red emergency backups and the shadows they cast were long and deep. Reggie's knuckles were white from the tightness of the grip he held his pistol in. Since the way appeared to be clear, he got moving.

He headed back through the Drake Complex towards the lift that would take him up into the sprawling mansion above it. Reggie's heart was thundering inside of his chest. He could feel it throbbing in his ears as he crept along the dimly lit corridor towards his destination. Reggie came to a stop as he heard the sickening, wet sound of smacking lips from somewhere around the bend that was ahead of him. Ever so cautiously, Reggie risked a peek around it. He saw the twisted, horrid form of a sea ape. Its ape-like upper body was bent over the crumpled, ravaged body of a dead soldier. The thing's lips were smeared with the soldier's blood and its hands tore hungrily at the man's flesh, ripping away entire sections of red meat that the thing crammed into its mouth. Ducking his head back so the thing had no chance of seeing him, Reggie sucked in a deep breath. The soldier had to have been part of a rescue team sent into evac the island by the Navy ship Reggie had been hoping was really more than just a rumor. The dead soldier was proof that it was. That meant there was help out there already on the island, all he had to do was find the rest of the rescue team and they could get him the hell out of here. . . assuming any of the rescue team was still alive.

The Sea Ape wasn't much of a threat out of the water for someone who knew what they were dealing with and it didn't have the natural body armor of the Mermen. Reggie could see that the creature was badly hurt despite the fury with which it was chowing down on the dead soldier. He came around the bend in the corridor, raising his pistol in a two handed grip, the barrel of the weapon aimed at the Sea Ape. Its wounded head jerked around towards him. The soldier looked to have put three rounds into its forehead already. It was amazing that the thing was still alive. Only the thick bone of its upper skull had saved its life. Knowing better than to waste bullets shooting at the Sea Ape's head, Reggie lowered his aim, letting loose a trio of rounds that tore into the monster's side and back. Bright red blood erupted from where the bullets entered the softer parts of the Sea Ape's body. The thing howled in pain, its body jerking about with each shot, and then promptly died. Its body collapsed onto the corridor floor and lay there in a growing puddle of its own blood. Reggie rushed to move the thing's corpse out of his way so that he could get to the soldier. The man was dead and beyond help but he knew there would be a radio or some kind of comm. unit on him.

"Hold it right there," a gruff voice barked at Reggie. He craned his head around to see three heavily armed soldiers in full combat gear. Their weapons were aimed at him, and from the expressions they wore, none of them would think twice about blowing him given half a reason. They looked to have been through just as much hell as he had.

"Put that gun on the floor next you, slowly," the soldier who was clearly the squad's C.O. ordered.

Reggie carefully set his pistol down, raising his hands above his head. "Are you part of the rescue team?"

"How the hell does he know about us?" the largest of the soldiers huffed at the C.O.

The C.O. ignored him, keeping his attention focused on Reggie. "Yes, we're the rescue team. I'm Corporal Anthony. The big guy is called Barrett and that's Cody. Now, mind telling us who you are exactly?"

"My name is Reggie. . . Reggie Byrne," he stammered. "I was part of this complex's security force."

"You guys sure did a bang up job here," the big soldier named Barrett snorted.

"Barrett!" Corporal Anthony snapped. "Stow that crap. I hear something like that again and I'll have you up on report. Can't you see this guy's been through hell too?"

"Hell," Reggie muttered and then began to speak louder. "Hell's a good way to put it. It's like that's what has been unleashed on this island."

"Reggie, are there. . .?" Corporal Anthony started.

The security man was already shaking his head in the negative. "No way. From what I saw at the party, everyone there was torn apart in a matter of minutes. If anyone did manage to get out of that massacre, you can bet the monsters have hunted them down by now."

"And you're certain of that?" Corporal Anthony pressed him.

"I'm a human like you, not God . . . but yeah, I am

as sure as I can be," Reggie said.

"Then how the hell are you still alive?" Barrett grumbled.

"My boss and I. . ." Reggie grimaced at the image of Rachel's corpse that reared up in his head. "We were both armed at the party. Knowing what we were up against and this complex as well as we do, I guess that tipped the odds in our favor. Cleary not enough though or she'd be with me right now."

"I am sorry for your loss," Cody frowned.

"Forget it," Reggie shrugged. "I'm sure trying to. There'll be time deal with all that later. Our focus needs to be on getting out of here alive while we still can."

"What's that supposed to mean?" Corporal Anthony raised an eyebrow. "While we still can? You say that as if you know something we don't."

"I know a bloody well lot more than you do about this place, what's been let loose, and what's about to be," Reggie answered. "Trust me. You've got a ship out there, right?"

Corporal Anthony nodded.

Reggie looked him directly in the eyes, "Then we should really get moving, don't ya think?"

****

"Fragging look at them out there," Flanigan shook his head, staring at the monitor screens which showed feeds from the area surrounding the Drake mansion. "It's like they're gearing up for war or something."

Brin couldn't argue with Flanigan's observation. There were mermen everywhere and the number of them carrying weapons had increased dramatically. What they were armed with varied wildly from one merman to the next. Some clutched spears that looked to be fashioned out of broken tree limbs or bits of wood torn from the mansion walls. Others had made sharp white knives and short swords forged hastily from the bones of their earlier victims. Brin's mind had been struggling with the question of how there were so many of the mermen but he knew now. It wasn't just the few dozen or so that Drake had imprisoned inside the depths of the complex below his mansion. Those that had escaped it were summoning more of their kind from the waves. One of the most outlying cameras showed several of the creatures standing on the beach blowing into large conch horns. It was clear the creatures were out for blood and wanted vengeance. The poor bastards they had torn to shreds and fed on at Drake's party apparently hadn't been enough to slack their bloodlust. Sooner or later, the things were going to realize that there was a warship floating out and when they did. . . well, Brin didn't really want to think about that. The U.S.S. Safeguard would never see the things coming. Hell, its commanding officer wouldn't even believe things like them could exist until they were on the deck of his ship directly engaged with his men.

"Brin," Flanigan said, snapping the specialist out of his dark thoughts.

"What, man?" Brin asked, rubbing at his eyes. "I got a lot going on right now."

"Really?" Flanigan spat at him. "I never would have guessed!"

Sighing, Brin stopped his eyes from darting from one screen to another and looked directly at Flanigan.

"I think we're going to have to admit we've lost this one," Flannigan told him.

"I would say that's pretty obvious," Brin frowned.

"You're not listening to me, Brin," Flanigan said. "I mean we're screwed if we stay here much longer. Those things are going to find a way in to get at us and you know it."

"But Corporal Anthony and. . ." Brin started.

"To Hell with the Corporal and his squad, man," Flanigan snapped. "We got to think about us at this point. If we don't, we're going to end up like the old man. Frag, it may be too late already."

"We can't just leave them, Flanigan," Brin argued. "That's not how we do things, you. . ."

"Screw you too then, Brin," Flanigan spat. "You want to sit here and die, that's on you. I am getting the hell out before things get any worse out there."

"And how are you going to do that?" Brin challenged him. "The Safeguard can't send an extraction bird right now A hole! The winds are crazy out there."

Brin heard a sharp click as Flanigan readied the rifle in his hands and then pointed its barrel at him. "Oh you'll get them to send in a bird, Brin. I've got faith in you buddy because if you don't, I'll splatter that big brain of yours all over the floor of this room."

Fresh beads of sweat formed on Brin's forehead as he stared at Flanigan. He could see something wasn't right in his fellow soldier's eyes. Flanigan had been slipping for a while, with the ups and downs of a rollercoaster ride, since they'd sealed themselves up in this room. Brin didn't doubt that Flannigan was far enough gone to make good on his threat. There was nothing else he could do anyway. His own rifle lay on the tabletop next to him but the weapon might as well have been on the moon. If he went for it that would be like signing his own death warrant. And Brin was no gunfighter, going for the pistol on his hip would be equally as useless. He'd be dead before the weapon cleared its holster.

"Okay," Brin said quietly. "Okay, man. I'll try."

"You damn well better do a lot more than try, man," Flanigan warned.

"The stuff in this room isn't really set up to reach anything not on this island, Flanigan," Brin explained. "I'll have to use our gear and even that's going to have a hard time getting a signal out through the latest round of weather that's rolled in.

"Safeguard, this is SAR Alpha. Please respond," Brin said through his personal long range, radio. Flanigan kept his rifle's aim centered squarely on the specialist's forehead. The only answer that came back was the crackle of static.

"The Rescue and Redeemer are out there too," Flanigan said.

Brin shook his head and sighed. "Sure they are but. . ."

"Get someone on damn it, Brin. I ain't kidding around here," Flanigan scowled, gritting his teeth.

"This is SAR Alpha, requesting emergency evac!" Brin yelled desperately in his radio, inwardly praying that someone would respond before Flanigan made good on his threat.

"This is Safeguard," a stern, female voice answered. "Emergency evac is unavailable at this time. Over."

"Fragging hell!" Brin screamed. "This island has been completely overrun by hostiles, Safeguard. We need evac now!"

There was a long pause. Brin and Flanigan watched each other closely until the Safeguard finally responded again.

"Copy that, SAR 1," the female voice told them. "Scrambling a Seahawk now. ETA in twenty, planned evac coordinates. Over. VTOL is currently grounded due to tech issues."

"Understood," Brin said back to her. "We'll be there."

"What the Hell, Brin?" Flanigan asked, still looking to be on the verge of blowing out his brain. "The extraction point is. . ."

"The roof of this mansion," Brin nodded, finishing for him. "Yeah, I know."

"You should have. . ." Flanigan started.

Brin found the courage to stop Flanigan there. "I got you birds coming in, you bastard! That's what you asked for!"

"But. . ." Flanigan frowned.

"But crap," Brin said firmly. "You and I both knew we would have to find our own way up there when you aimed your gun at me, man. There was no way in hell they would risk sending in another rescue team. We just told them this place was overrun by hostiles, Flanigan."

Flanigan lowered his rifle, getting up from his seat. "We're cool, Brin."

"Frag you, Flanigan," Brin glared up at him. "I'd say we're a hell of a way from being cool."

"Suit yourself, man," Flanigan grunted. "The thing is. . .it's time for us to figure out how to get to the roof. The clock is ticking. Those copters will be here in less than twenty."

"Brin!" a shout rang out from the room's comm. console. The voice belonged to Corporal Anthony. Brin reached to respond but Flanigan grabbed his hand before it could touch the console.

"What the hell do you think you're doing? Don't answer him!" Flanigan snapped.

"Frag you, Flanigan!" Brin snapped, left hand slipping down along his side, beneath the top of console he was sitting at. "I'm not leaving them to die here. Besides, we'll need all the firepower we can get to make it up to the roof through those mermen out there."

"Get your arse up, Brin," Flanigan warned. "I can't make it to the roof without you."

"Then I guess you're not going anywhere either," Brin shot back.

Flanigan jerked up his rifle at him but this time, he was ready. Brin's pistol whipped up, aimed right back at him.

"Brin!" Corporal Anthony's voice called out over the comm. again. "We've made it to the lift below your position but it's not responding. I need you to make it operable! We've got a really nasty *thing* on our six and closing in fast."

Holding his pistol steady towards Flanigan, Brin answered, "On it, Corporal."

"Don't you. . ." Flanigan started but it was too late. Brin had already stabbed the control that returned power to the lift below.

"It's working now, sir," Brin said over the comm. "Give it another go."

Both Brin and Flanigan heard the lift kick into

gear, rising upward towards the room they were holed up in.

"Damn you," Flanigan spat but he didn't take a shot at Brin. Instead, he lowered his weapon again, defeated.

****

Corporal Anthony looked around at the others inside the lift with him. Cody was sweating like crazy, his eyes flittering about as if half expecting a monster to somehow come out of nowhere at them. Barrett was holding his rifle at the ready but otherwise gave the appearance that it was just another day on the job. And Reggie, the security man they'd found in the bowels of the complex below and brought with them, was chewing loudly on some gum he'd fished out of his pocket. They were all on their way up out of the complex now, but that sure as hell didn't mean they were safe yet.

The lift door opened into the room where Brin and Flanigan had holed up in not long after the rescue team arrived on the island. At a glance, Corporal Anthony could see that things weren't right with the two of them. Brin and Flanigan were watching each other closely.

"Corporal," Flanigan greeted them with a nod.

"Sitrep," Corporal Anthony demanded.

"Everyone else is dead, sir," Brin informed him. "We've made contact with the fleet and a group of extraction copters are inbound. E.T.A. in eighteen minutes."

"Wow," Reggie looked in Barrett's direction with a smug expression. "Guess you guys really screwed up too, huh?"

"No one expected there to be real freaking monsters everywhere on this island!" Barrett protested.

"Then what did you expect to find here?" Reggie challenged him.

Corporal Anthony spoke up, interrupting. "That doesn't matter. Nothing matters but getting out of here alive, people."

"Amen to that," Flanigan smiled.

Eying Brin, Corporal Anthony frowned. "Anything else you'd like to report to me, Specialist Brin?"

Brin shook his head. "No sir. I don't think so."

"Understood," Corporal Anthony nodded. "I assume the LZ is still the same."

"Yes sir," Flanigan said, pointing at the screen which showed live feeds from both the mansion exterior and interior, "And that's the problem. In order to get up there, we have to go through them."

There were more Mermen on the screens than Corporal Anthony could even attempt to make a guess at their number.

"What the hell?" Reggie gawked. "Where did they all come from? Mr. Drake didn't have anywhere near that many held here."

"Once those held here got free, I believe they began to summon others of their kind to this island," Brin answered. "In truth, we've seen it happening. Not long before you arrived, a giant wave of them came ashore and started spreading out in every direction. The camera in that area went down, or maybe was destroyed, it's hard to say, but regardless it's a safe bet to assume that wave was only the first of many."

Corporal Anthony grunted. "Well, fighting our way up to the roof isn't an option. We'd be overwhelmed and torn apart before we made if off this floor."

He turned to Reggie, "This is your turf. Is there another way of getting up there?"

Reggie shrugged. "My job was security within the complex. I'm not that familiar with this mansion."

"Hold up!" Brin suddenly exclaimed. "I might just have us a way."

Everyone watched Brin as the tech went to work at the closest console. His brow furrowed in concentration, Brin's fingers danced over the keyboard, pulling up schematics of the mansion. He projected a map of it onto the room's main screen so they could all see it. "I think our best bet isn't in finding a different path to the roof but in coming up with a distraction."

Brin stabbed his finger onto the map.

"What the heck is that?" Barrett asked.

"Frag me," Reggie muttered. "That's the drone storage shed, isn't it?"

Brin nodded.

"Someone care to explain to us non-techies?" Corporal Anthony frowned.

"Our security here. . ." Reggie answered, "we sometimes used drones to keep an eye on the surrounding ocean or to send into the containment cells below."

"Still not getting you," Barrett shrugged.

"Those drones are remote controlled," Reggie grinned. "If your man here could. . ."

"I can access their systems," Brin smiled. "Firing them up and getting them moving won't be a problem at all. What will be a problem is getting them out of that shed and to where they can help us."

"No," Reggie spoke up. "It won't. Some of the drones in there are weaponized, pretty heavily armed."

"Really?" Brin seemed pleasantly surprised.

"Yep, they had to be," Reggie confirmed. "Tap into the systems of the Mark XIIIs."

Brin did as Reggie suggested, his eyes lighting up with excitement at the schematics filling the screen of his console.

"Frag yeah," Brin nodded. "We're in business. I can use one of the armed drones to shoot a way out for the others and bring them here. Once they are, I can create one hell of a diversion that should draw the attention of the mermen, most of them anyway, from anything we're up to."

"How long will it take to break out the drones and get them here?" Corporal Anthony asked.

"Three minutes, give or take," Brin told him.

"I am loving this plan," Flanigan cackled.

Corporal Anthony looked around at the others. "Okay. Brin, can you maintain control of those drones while you're on the move?"

"Shouldn't be a problem, sir," Brin smiled. "I've got a handheld I can tie them into."

"Good," Corporal Anthony nodded. "We've lost enough folks already."

"The drones are inbound," Brin said loudly. He'd called up a feed from one of the exterior cameras that showed an image of the mansion's main doors.

"Get ready to move out, people," Corporal Anthony ordered.

Outside, a dozen drones came buzzing through the sky towards the mansion. The snarling faces of the mermen milling about around the main doors rose towards them. The creatures had apparently seen the drones or others like them inside of their containment area. Reggie had said that the drones had been used in such a fashion. The mermen didn't appear to think the drones a threat, though one of them did lift the trident it was carrying, shaking the weapon skyward at them. It was at that moment Brin clicked the drones into attack mode. The drones broke their current formation, splitting into groups of three except for a single drone that flew directly into the group of mermen gathered outside the doorway. It streaked downward like a missile, detonating among them in a fiery blast that sent shards of shrapnel flying into the scaled bodies of the mermen. Shrieks of pain and splashing black blood filled the air. The other drones took up firing positions with two groups facing away from the mansion and the last aiming their weapons through the blown apart doorway. Their small machine guns roared to life, barrels spinning beneath the main bodies of the drones, hosing the mermen with hot lead. More of the mermen squealed. Most of the mermen near the mansion scurried for any kind of cover they could find. Those approaching from the oceanside were stopped in their tracks, many of them ripped to shreds in the storm of bullets.

Everything appeared to be working like a charm. Corporal Anthony gave the signal for Flanigan to throw open the control room's door. Barrett and Cody were the first through it. Everyone had armed up for the running fight to get to the roof. Barrett had traded his normal rifle for a pump action shotgun. The weapon boomed, blowing a gaping hole in the center of a merman's chest while Cody's M27 chattered on full auto. The merman struck by

Cody's rounds staggered, driven backwards, as its body jerked about. Finally, the creature collapsed to the floor and lay there with a puddle of black blood spreading out around it.

Flanigan and Reggie were the next out in the open area of the mansion's foyer. The thundering cacophony of the drones' gunfire and the shrieks of the mermen hurt Reggie's ears. The soldiers had given him an M27 rifle and he put it to use blazing away at a merman who was retreating from the fury of the drones' continued bombardment of his kin both inside and outside of the mansion. The shrill voices of the mermen were almost too much for Flanigan to take at such close range. He loosed his pain and anger on them with his M27 on full auto, hosing two of the creatures that had more stumbled into his path, retreating from the weapons of the drones, than moved there to block him. His M27 blazed away as its rounds tore into their scale-covered forms.

Seeing that the others were out of the control room and moving, Corporal Anthony knew it was time for him to get moving. Only Brin remained in the room with him. The specialist was intently focused on the handheld device he was using to control the drones.

"Time to go!" Corporal Anthony yelled at Brin.

The specialist looked up from the screen of his device and gave a quick nod. Corporal Anthony watched Brin keying in whatever the hell it took to make the drones continue to attack on their own and then tuck the handheld into a pocket of his jacket. Brin grabbed up his rifle and hurried towards the door where Corporal Anthony was waiting for him.

Cody and Barrett had reached the stairs leading upwards off the mansion's ground floor. Flanigan and Reggie were closing in fast on their heels. So far, things were going perfectly to plan. They hadn't lost anyone despite the dozens of mermen that were close enough to rush them.

The mermen were still under relentless and brutal attack by the weaponized drones. One of them was done just taking it though. The merman roared, rising up from the cover of an overturned desk in the foyer and rushed forward, throwing its trident. It struck the drone firing at the section of the massive room where the merman was. The trident pierced the drone with the sound of crunching metal in a shower of sparks. The drone veered sideways, crashing into the wall. It exploded there in a fiery blast as the ammo in its twin machine guns blew. That single merman and his act of courage changed everything. The other mermen rallied, getting into the fight against the drones, as the merman who had taken out of the drone sprinted across the massive room, dodging bullets as best as possible as he ran. The merman still took several hits that sent black blood splattering into the air but ignored the pain they caused, not even slowing down. The merman leaped at the drone he'd closed in on, grabbing onto it. The drone was roughly the size of a shield and weighed around fifty pounds with the weapons and ammo it was carrying. Still, that was nothing to the merman. He snatched it easily from the air, yanking it down to ground level, and flung the drone onto the floor at his feet. It shattered there, exploding apart into thousands of pieces but not before extracting its vengeance on him. The drone's guns had wracked the merman's body with its machine guns as he had pulled it from the air. The merman was already dead as the shrapnel from the blast of its death ripped through him, tearing his body apart.

The drones were taken out one by one as the mermen fought back in force. Hurled tridents knocked them from the sky and air inside the mansion where they hovered in their firing positions. Corporal Anthony realized just how much trouble he and the others were about to be in.

****

"Oh frag me," Flanigan sucked in a breath as he saw the mermen turning their attention to him and Reggie. Cody and Barrett had already reached the second floor above them and were laying down covering fire for them. Corporal Anthony and Brin were still trying to make their way to the stairs.

"Watch it!" Reggie shouted as a merman sprung up from beside the stairs and launched itself at

Flanigan. Ducking out of the clawed hand that swiped at his face, Flanigan emptied what remained of his rifle's magazine into the creature. The merman was flung backwards as the bullets from the M27 opened up its guts. They spilled from its abdomen, splashing onto the floor in a splattering mess of black gore. The creature dragged long strands of blood slick intestines in front of it continuing to reel backwards until finally collapsing.

Reggie started to bring up his rifle to take aim at the mermen approaching from the mansion's destroyed main doors but before he could a merman took him by surprise coming around the base of the stairs at him. The thing's razor clawed fingers closed on his M27, tearing it from his hands. The gun clattered across the floor of the foyer as the creature threw it away. The merman showed Reggie its mouthful of fang-like teeth, shrieking at him. Reggie shot his hands out, palms flat, at the merman, trying to push it back and put some space between them. He felt the cold, slimy scales of the monster's chest against his skin as he struck it but despite using all his strength in the effort, the merman was too strong to be moved. It grabbed each of his arms, one in each hand, and bent them at unnatural angles away from its chest. Reggie screamed as the bones in his arms snapped, splintering beneath his flesh. Jagged bits of white erupted just below each of his elbows.

Flanigan saw what was happening to Reggie but

didn't give a crap. All that mattered to him was making it to the top of the stairs alive. He scampered up them, moving as fast as he could without looking back.

Corporal Anthony and Brin had no choice but to keep moving for the stairs. Stopping or turning back were nothing but death sentences now that the mermen's attention was on them. Brin opened on two fast approaching mermen, spraying the creatures with hot lead. One took several rounds to its chest, the thing's shrill cries rising in pitch as it was flung backwards by their impact. The other merman dropped instantly to the floor, head snapping back atop its neck. Brin had landed a lucky shot, a round smacking right in the center of its forehead. For every merman that fell though, it seemed like two more took their place, chasing after them or moving to try to block their path.

"Move it!" Corporal Anthony yelled, glancing over his shoulder at Brin, urging the specialist on.

As Corporal Anthony picked up his own speed, racing for the stairs, a merman came plowing into him from his right side like a linebacker. His feet left the floor as the two of them spun through the air on their way to crash hard on the wood beneath them. There was a crunching sound of fracturing bone as Corporal Anthony felt his right leg break from how the creature landed on top of him. Its claws raked over the flesh of his arms and chest. He lashed out from the pain and in desperation to keep the merman from sinking its yellow teeth into his neck. Corporal Anthony's elbow slammed into the thing's lower jaw with all the strength he could muster. The blow struck at just the right angle to break it. The merman's upper torso jerked up and away from him, giving Corporal Anthony the chance he needed to draw the pistol holstered on his hip. His rifle had been knocked from his hands from his impact with the floor. Before he could get off a shot with the pistol though, Brin appeared over him, pressing the barrel of his M27 to the side of the raging merman's skull. The specialist pulled the trigger of the rifle unleashing a burst of rounds that blew the creature's head apart in a shower of gore and bone fragments. Its body flopped forward, threatening to come straight down on top of him, as Corporal Anthony watched Brin kick the creature's headless corpse. The kick was enough to get its dead body off him. Corporal Anthony wasted no time in shoving himself up onto his feet. He grunted, nearly blacking out from the pain that surged through him from his broken leg. Brin caught him, helping him to stay up. Corporal Anthony flashed a smile at the specialist, believing for a moment that they just might make it up the stairs and escape this hellish island alive.

Brin was ripped away from him, leaving Corporal Anthony reeling sideways, trying to keep his balance with only a single good leg to stand on. His eyes went wide at the sight of the mermen that had grabbed hold of Brin from behind. Their claws sunk into the specialist's flesh, drawing blood, as they pulled him in between them and other mermen rushed up, swarming Brin as they pulled him down onto the floor. Suddenly, all Corporal Anthony could see of the specialist was Brin's kicking legs as they thrashed about wildly. Brin's pain-wracked wails were like something out of a nightmare. They rose sharply in intensity and then went quickly silent.

Corporal Anthony managed to right himself, limping onward for the stairs. He reached their bottom, looking up at Cody and Barrett. There was no sign of Flanigan. God only knew where that bastard had gone. It was clear now just what kind of A hole he really was and Corporal Anthony regretted not shooting the fragger in the head before they had left the control room.

Both Cody and Barrett came down the stairs, guns blazing, trying to drive the swarming mermen back.

"No!" Corporal Anthony barked, motioning for them to get back up the stairs. Neither of them was listening to him though. He felt Cody take hold of him, pulling him up.

"Come on, sir!" Cody shouted. "We're going to get you out of here!"

Realizing that continuing his protests would only endanger them all, Corporal Anthony limped along next to Cody as he was led, half dragged, up the stairs. Behind them, Barrett's shotgun thundered, punching a hole through a merman's rib cage in an explosion of black blood.

As he and Cody reached the top of the stairs, Corporal Anthony heard Barrett's deep voice crying out below them and knew that the big man had lost the battle to hold back the hungry creatures that were coming after them.

"Run for it, sir!" Cody screamed, shoving him on. "Barrett needs help!"

Corporal Anthony's hand snapped outward trying to grab Cody and keep him from turning back but he wasn't fast enough. Cody was already bounding back the way they had come, his weapon roaring on full auto. It didn't take a genius to know the kid had just killed himself. The numbers of the mermen were too great for any kind of heroics. There was no saving anyone anymore. All that was left was claws, razor teeth, and painful death. Determined not to let Cody's sacrifice be in vain as the kid's death was going to buy him some time, Corporal Anthony limped across the second floor towards the lift that Flanigan was standing in front of. The lift's doors hissed open and Flanigan moved to step through them.

"Hold it," Corporal Anthony shouted, "or I'll blow your fragging brains out, Trooper!"

Flanigan's head swung around, the man's beady eyes glaring in his direction. It looked as if the bastard was actually considering taking a shot at him as Corporal Anthony continued limping close, the barrel of his pistol aimed at Flanigan.

"Hurry the hell up then!" Flanigan barked.

Corporal Anthony reached him and the two of them dove into the lift together. Its doors hissed shut in their wake just before the mermen reached the lift.

"You damn bastard," Corporal Anthony snarled at Flanigan, his pistol still leveled at him.

Flanigan's rifle was now aimed right back at Corporal Anthony.

The lift pinged as it reached the roof. The doors hissed open as both men flinched, swinging their weapons around in that direction. Wind and rain whipped inside the lift, splashing over them, large raindrops bursting against their skin. The extraction chopper was already waiting on the roof, its side gunner looking nervous, finger on the trigger of his .50 caliber mini-gun.

Corporal Anthony and Flanigan hurried out of the lift, moving across the roof through the storm, towards the helicopter. As soon as they were aboard, the chopper rose into the sky, streaking away from the mansion.

****

Captain Walter Herbert stood in the CIC of the USS Safeguard. The extraction chopper had touched down on deck half an hour ago. The only two survivors from the search and rescue force were taken straight to the ship's sickbay. Corporal Anthony was badly injured from what he had heard so Captain Herbert ordered the other survivor, Flanigan, to brief him about what was found on the island. . .and below it. Flanigan's story would have been utterly unbelievable except for the fact that there was a hell of a lot of proof to back it up- video footage, strange activity in the water surrounding the island that his techs couldn't begin to explain in a rational way, not to mention that what the extraction chopper's pilots taken video footage of from the air. That footage had shaken Herbert to his core as he watched it. The beaches of the island and the area of it where the Drake mansion was swarming with. . . things, creatures that Flanigan swore were literal mermen. Whatever the things were, they sure as hell weren't human. Captain Herbert had been briefed to expect things akin to monsters on the island when his small fleet was ordered to come out here and play watchdog.

Flanigan stood not far away and looking very much like he was eager to be dismissed. Either that or the trooper was waiting for him to give the order that everyone in the CIC figured was coming.

"Commence fire," Captain Herbert barked. "Rapid and continuous. I want everything on that island turned to ash."

All three of the destroyers in his fleet opened up

on the island. Their main guns boomed in a cacophony of thunderous fury as missiles streaked away from each ship, blazing towards the distant island. The night was lit up by the eruption of spreading flames that gleamed brightly through the falling rain.

As Captain Herbert watched the island being pounded and decimated, a commotion rose up outside the CIC.

"Stop! You can't. . ." one of the security officers outside it shouted but then his voice was cut off. The door to the CIC was flung open in that moment, as Captain Herbert and Flanigan both saw the security officer's collapsing body and Corporal Anthony forcing his way in to join them.

"What the hell have you done?" Corporal Anthony raged.

"Corporal!" Captain Herbert yelled in shock and anger.

"You idiots," Corporal Anthony was shaking his head though he had halted his mad charge towards the Captain.

"I'm willing to forgive you this outburst, Corporal, given the hell you've just endured, but that's rather enough now," Captain Herbert cautioned him.

The head of the Safeguard's sonar officer, Thomas, swung up from the screen of his station. "Captain!"

Captain Herbert whipped around to face Thomas.

"What?"

"There's something. . .happening beneath the Drake Island, sir," Thomas informed him.

"How could you let him do this?" Corporal Anthony challenged Flanigan. If he'd still had his sidearm, Corporal Anthony would have shot the bastard right then and there, consequences be damned. Too many people had already died because of the man's selfishness and cowardice.

"Restrain the Corporal before he does something he'll regret!" Captain Herbert ordered the security officers outside the doors of the CIC. They hurried in, grabbing hold of Corporal Anthony. At first, he tried to break free of their hold on him but quickly stopped, staring at Captain Herbert.

"You've killed us all," Corporal Anthony said, his voice calmer and filled with the tone of bitter acceptance.

"Thomas?" Captain Herbert asked now that the Corporal had been dealt with.

"I've never seen anything like what's happening beneath the Drake Island, sir. It's as if part of the complex under it has just broken off but it's not drifting, Captain, it's CBDR and picking up speed towards the fleet."

"What the hell?" Captain Herbert gawked at Thomas. "That's impossible. Could our attack on the island's surface have triggered some kind of defensive response from the complex?"

"You don't understand, sir," Thomas shook his head. "The contact that is inbound, it's not the size of munitions. The thing is almost the size of the island itself."

"God help us," Corporal Anthony muttered, now knowing for sure his instinct about what was happening was right.

"Is there something you want to tell me, Mr. Flanigan?" Captain Herbert glared at the soldier.

Flanigan was pale now, as if he too had slowly come to the same conclusion that Corporal Anthony had.

"Tell him about cell 13," Corporal Anthony spat at Flanigan.

"The contact speed is now approaching twenty-five knots," Thomas reported. "And still increasing. It's on a ramming course, heading directly for the Rescue."

Of the three ships in Captain Herbert's fleet, the Rescue was the closest to the island. It lay between the Safeguard and whatever was coming at them.

"Captain Miller has initiated evasive maneuvers, sir," Thomas added.

"The Rescue and Redeemer are requesting permission to engage the contact," the communications officer, Munro, butted in.

"Just what the frag are we up against here, Corporal?" Captain Herbert demanded, not bothering to ask Flanigan. His trust in the man had been shattered.

"Hell itself, unleashed and hungry," Corporal Anthony answered coldly.

Captain Herbert didn't have time to press him for a better answer. The contact was closing too fast. "Tell Miller and Gibson they are free to engage the contact with whatever means are needed to ensure their safety. And Zdarsky," he added to the Safeguard's helmsman, "Get us moving. Maximum speed out of that thing's path."

The Rescue and Redeemer, despite their names, were better equipped to deal with the contact than the Safeguard. They were both full out destroyers and made for contact whereas the Safeguard was a hybrid ship in terms of her class, focused more on straight up search and rescue than combat.

"Yes sir!" Zdarsky answered. The Safeguard lurched as her engines engaged at full power.

With the Safeguard moving and the rest of the fleet ready to deal with the approaching contact, Captain Herbert returned his attention to Corporal Anthony.

"Tell me what that thing out there is, Corporal," Captain Herbert pressed.

"Why don't you ask Flanigan?" the Corporal grunted.

"I am asking you," Captain Herbert frowned.

"Beneath that island was the Drake Complex," Corporal Anthony said. "And beneath it was

Containment Cell 13. That cell contained the largest and most dangerous of Drake's little collection of monsters. According to Specialist Brin before he died, Drake called the creature in that cell an Octa. I don't know where or how Drake came to call the monster that but Brin said there was another name for it. The ancient Greeks called the thing in that cell a Kraken . . .and you've just released it."

Captain Herbert stared at the Corporal for a long moment before he spoke again. He wanted to think that Corporal Anthony was insane, that the man's time on the island had broken his mind, anything but accepting what he'd just been told and had no choice but to believe given the evidence in front of him. The contact that was coming at his fleet surely had to be exactly what Corporal Anthony claimed it was. Nothing else could be so large and yet so fragging fast. It defied reality, mocked rational thought, but Captain Herbert knew it was true nonetheless.

"The contact's speed has increased to thirty knots, Captain," Thomas called out. "ETA to the Rescue is now less than two minutes."

****

Aboard the Rescue, Captain Miller stood in the center of her CIC, watching his crew scramble to carry out his latest round of orders. Taking evasive maneuvers hadn't done crap. The approaching contact had matched each of their course shifts and was steadily maintaining a CBDR heading with them. The Rescue's ship to ship harpoon missiles fired. She had two sets of four tube launcher clusters. Two missiles were launched from each at the approaching contact. In addition, the Rescue's main guns took aim at the contact, locking into firing solutions, before unleashing a series of thunderous booms as they fired in rapid succession. The Redeemer began firing as well, though she was throwing everything but the kitchen sink at the contact like the Rescue was. Only a single missile from each of her forward launchers blazed into the air.

The harpoon missiles from both ships reached the area of the ocean where the contact was inbound, splashing downward into the water. There was a series of explosions, like firecrackers on a string going off, one by one, as the missiles detonated. In their wake, the heavy shells from the Rescue's main guns struck, rippling and tearing at the water with equal fury.

"Rogers, report! Contact status," Captain Miller barked.

"Multiple direct hits, sir!" Roger told him. "With the contact so close to the surface the harpoons had to do some serious damage."

"They didn't," Jenkins, the Rescue's XO cut in, "That thing out there hasn't even slowed down. It's still CBDR and coming in fast!"

"Evasive maneuvers!" Captain Miller shouted at the top of his lungs though he knew there was no chance of escaping what was coming. "Gunners! Keep that damned thing off of us."

The Rescue's deck guns continued to thunder. Water flew skyward as their heavy rounds hammered at the inbound contact.

"Captain!" Roger yelled, motioning for Miller to hurry over to his station. "We've got visual!"

"God in heaven help us," Captain Miller muttered as he saw the image on the screen of Roger's console. The thing was like something out of a nightmare. . .something straight out of the worst sort of naval myths. There was no questioning what the creature was to Miller's mind though he couldn't bring himself to say its name aloud. He could feel the same fear that his sea going ancestors must have at the sight of the beast. The creature was easily over a mile long and very squid-like in its appearance. The barrage of harpoon missiles and fire from the Rescue's guns had inflicted some horrid wounds upon it that leaked black blood but even as he watched the monster, Captain Miller could see those wounds healing before his eyes. There wasn't going to be any stopping the creature. The Rescue alone didn't have that sort of firepower at her disposal and the Redeemer couldn't get a clean firing solution for her deck guns given how close the thing was now. If the Redeemer opened fire, her weapons were sure to hit the Rescue too.

The Kraken's speed was close to fifty knots when the great beast struck the Rescue. It rammed directly into the ship's magazine. The Rescue exploded, blowing apart, bits of her shattered hull spun through the air away from her main mass.

****

Captain Gibson's eyes bugged as she watched the Rescue go up in flames. Her ship, the Redeemer, was on an intercept course for the creature, something she now regretted ordering. The Redeemer's deck guns had opened up on the impossibly large monster. Captain Gibson felt a surge of pride at the gunners' actions, not that the barrage of fire they were pouring into the massive creature that had shifted its own course and was now coming directly at the Redeemer.

She didn't give a damn what anyone else was calling the thing coming at her ship. To her, it was a freaking Kraken. There was a long trail of black in the Kraken's wake. Captain Gibson was sure that the black was the Kraken's blood. The ships of the fleet had shot the hell out of the thing. She couldn't help but wonder how the giant beast wasn't dead. Sure, it was big as hell but if it bled, then surely it could die, at least that was what she told herself. . . and she was determined to do her best to send the big bastard to hell.

"Torpedoes are loaded and armed!" her Xo told her.

"Lock onto inbound contact and fire!" Captain Miller snapped. "Let's show this thing you don't screw with the United States Navy."

Two Mark 50 torpedoes shot off the deck mounted launchers into the water. They sped away from the Redeemer on a direct course for the approaching Kraken. The great beast made no effort to dodge them. The Kraken simply plowed through them as they detonated, seeming as if the blasts were no more than gnat bites to it.

"Bring us about hard to port!" Captain Gibson yelled at the helm. "Maximum speed!"

The Redeemer banked hard in the water, changing course, her deck guns still roaring. The cacophony of destruction was deafening. Her CIWS had shifted down in their turrets to target the approaching Kraken as well. Their high-pitched chattering only added to the noise of the battle. But Captain Gibson knew this wasn't really a battle. The Kraken wasn't shooting back at them. It was merely continuing to close, taking everything that they could throw at it, and shrugging it off.

Captain Gibson watched through the CIC's observation window as a shell slammed into the topside of the Kraken. Blood splashed upwards in an explosion of black gore. The Kraken didn't show any signs of even noticing. Its course remained steady.

The thing was at such close range now that the Redeemer's missile launchers were useless. The Phalanx CIWS and the larger DDG-81 guns were her only remaining defenses. Members of her crew scrambled about on her deck, carrying out their duties despite the impending doom that would soon be upon them.

The Redeemer's engines were howling, straining, pushed to their limits, as she sped through the water. Captain Miller knew the ship couldn't keep up this sort of speed much longer. They couldn't slow down though. If they did, they were dead. Hell, they were dead anyway but Captain Miller was determined that if she couldn't kill the fragging monster on their tail, she was at least going to make the bastard work to take them out.

There simply was no hope of escaping the beast or killing it.

"All hands brace for impact!" Captain Miller shouted over the Redeemer's internal communications system.

The Kraken struck the ship from aft. Part of the hull screeched as metal bent and was crushed inward as the Redeemer was partially lifted out of the water, the Kraken's massive form slipping beneath it. The destroyer splashed back down atop the waves.

"Damage report!" Captain Miller wailed, hauling herself. The impact had flung her over onto the metal floor. She was bruised and bleeding from a cut on her forehead where it had been slashed by the edge of the console on her way down. Even so, she was luckier than a lot of the others in the CIC. Entire systems had shorted out, blowing their consoles. For the crewmen and women stationed at them it was like having a grenade go off in front of their faces. People were lying all around the CIC, bleeding and screaming in pain. . . others unable to muster more than agonized moans.

Before anyone could answer Captain Miller, the Kraken rammed into the Redeemer again. The great beast had dived downwards in the water and now came back up like a missile, slamming into and through the Redeemer at midship. The destroyer broke in two, her separate halves being flung apart, and already beginning to sink. Captain Miller, like so many others aboard, didn't survive that second strike.

*****

Having seen what happened to the Rescue and the Redeemer, Captain Herbert knew just how ineffective engaging the Kraken with the Safeguard's weapons would be. Both of those ships were armed to the teeth destroyers and neither of them had seemed to more than make the Kraken angrier than it already was at being kept prisoner in the complex beneath Drake's island.

"We're fragging dead men!" Flanigan wailed,

seeing what had happened to the Redeemer and apparently coming to the same conclusion about the Safeguard being unable to stop the Kraken.

"Get that bastard out of here!" Captain Herbert ordered his security officers.

"What the hell, man?" Flanigan protested as they released Corporal Anthony and came towards him. He went for his sidearm, as he was still packing a 9mm pistol, but before he could draw it, one of the officers lunged at him. The security man's fist met Flanigan's jaw. The blow was enough to render Flanigan unconscious. The security officers caught him as he dropped, dragging his limp form out of the CIC.

Unlike the two destroyers, the Safeguard, after firing a few shots during the initial engagement with the Kraken, had turned tail and ran. It hadn't been a call Captain Herbert wanted to make but the Safeguard was the command ship and smallest vessel of the fleet. The Rescue and Redeemer were supposed to be her protective escorts. Though they had failed to stop the Kraken, the time the great beast had spent in destroying them had given the Safeguard a chance to put some distance between herself and it. Her engines were redlining from how hard they were being pushed as she fled but Captain Herbert knew there was no help coming. Not even fighters scrambled from the closest base could reach them in enough time to matter. The Safeguard was on her own. What bothered Captain Herbert in this moment was the fact that there was no visual sign of the massive creature.

Captain Herbert turned to his sonar officer, "Thomas?"

The sonar tech was frantic at his station. His brow was wet with sweat and his eyes bugging. "I . . .I don't know, sir. The creature seems to either have disappeared or. . . or something has knocked out our sonar."

Frowning, Captain Herbert marched across the CIC towards the sonar station. Corporal Anthony followed after him.

"I can't find anything wrong with the system, sir," Thomas said. "Everything checks out. It's like that thing just disappeared."

Captain Herbert looked over Thomas' shoulder at the sonar screen. He saw what was wrong with it instantly and nearly crapped himself. There wasn't anything truly wrong with the sonar. It was simply that the Kraken was directly below the Safeguard and that was all the system could pick up. The creature's mass was simply filling the entire screen and making it seem empty.

"Captain!" a crewman near the CIC's observation window cried out.

Both Captain Herbert and Corporal Anthony looked up, out the window, to see a gigantic tentacle come whipping up from the waves. It raised into the air above the Safeguard before coming crashing down onto her. The tentacle crushed everything on the deck under it as it struck, slashing downward into the interior of the ship. Everyone on the CIC was screaming as Captain Herbert stood, frozen in place, staring at the horrific scene outside. A second tentacle emerged from the water, striking and then wrapping around the Safeguard just as the first had.

"It's going to pull us under!" Corporal Anthony cried out in warning but there was nothing that anyone could do.

The Safeguard and everyone aboard her were yanked downward, beneath the waves. Water rushed into the ship, flooding the ship. Everything went dark as the Kraken dragged the Safeguard deeper and deeper towards the bottom of the ocean and even the sunlight above vanished from view.

Corporal Anthony felt coldness all around him as his lungs filled up. The last thing he saw before he closed his eyes, accepting his death, was Captain Herbert's corpse being carried past him by the rushing water that had filled the CIC.

END

AUTHOR BIO

Eric S Brown is the author of numerous book series including the Bigfoot War series, the Psi-Mechs Inc. series, the Kaiju Apocalypse series (with Jason Cordova), the Crypto-Squad series (with Jason Brannon), the Homeworld series (With Tony Faville and Jason Cordova), the Jack Bunny Bam series, and the A Pack of Wolves series. Some of his stand alone books include War of the Worlds plus Blood Guts and Zombies, Casper Alamo (with Jason Brannon), Sasquatch Island, Day of the Sasquatch, Bigfoot, Crashed, World War of the Dead, Last Stand in a Dead Land, Sasquatch Lake, Kaiju Armageddon, Megalodon, Megalodon Apocalypse, Kraken, Alien Battalion, The Last Fleet, and From the Snow They Came to name only a few. His short fiction has been published hundreds of times in the small press in beyond including markets like the Onward Drake and Black Tide Rising anthologies from Baen Books, the Grantville Gazette, the SNAFU Military horror anthology series, and Walmart World magazine. He has done the novelizations for such films as Boggy Creek: The Legend is True (Studio 3 Entertainment) and The Bloody Rage of Bigfoot (Great Lake films). The first book of his Bigfoot War series was adapted into a feature film by Origin Releasing in 2014. Werewolf Massacre at Hell's Gate was the second of his books to be adapted into film in 2015. Major Japanese publisher, Takeshobo, bought the reprint rights to his Kaiju Apocalypse series (with Jason Cordova) and the mass market, Japanese language version was released in late 2017. Ring of Fire Press has released a collected edition of his Monster Society stories (set in the New York Times Best-selling world of Eric Flint's 1632). In addition to his fiction, Eric also writes an award-winning comic book news column entitled "Comics in a Flash" as well a pop culture column for Altered Reality Magazine. Eric lives in North Carolina with his wife and two children where he continues to write tales of the hungry dead, blazing guns, and the things that lurk in the woods.

Check out other great
Sea Monster Novels!

Matt James
SUB-ZERO

The only thing colder than the Antarctic air is the icy chill of death... Off the coast of McMurdo Station, in the frigid waters of the Southern Ocean, a new species of Antarctic octopus is unintentionally discovered. Specialists aboard a state-of-the-art DARPA research vessel aim to apply the animal's "sub-zero venom" to one of their projects: An experimental painkiller designed for soldiers on the front lines. All is going according to plan until the ship is caught in an intense storm. The retrofitted tanker is rocked, and the onboard laboratory is destroyed. Amid the chaos, the lead scientist is infected by a strange virus while conducting the specimen's dissection. The scientist didn't die in the accident. He changed.

Alister Hodge
THE CAVERN

When a sink hole opens up near the Australian outback town of Pintalba, it uncovers a pristine cave system. Sam joins an expedition to explore the subterranean passages as paramedic support, hoping to remain unneeded at base camp. But, when one of the cavers is injured, he must overcome paralysing claustrophobia to dive pitch-black waters and squeeze through the bowels of the earth. Soon he will find there are fates worse than being buried alive, for in the abandoned mines and caves beneath Pintalba, there are ravenous teeth in the dark. As a savage predator targets the group with hideous ferocity, Sam and his friends must fight for their lives if they are ever to see the sun again.

Check out other great

Sea Monster Novels!

Robert J. Stava

NEPTUNES RECKONING

At the easternmost end of Long Island lies a seaside town known as Montauk. Ground Zero on the Eastern seaboard for all manner of conspiracy theories involving it's hidden Cold War military base, rumors of time-travel experiments and alien visitors... For renowned Naval historian William Vanek it's the where his grandfather's ship went down on a Top Secret mission during WWII code-named "Neptune's Reckoning". Together with Marine Biologist Daniel Cheung and disgraced French underwater explorer Arnaud Navarre, he's about to discover the truth behind the urban legends: a nightmare from beyond space and time that has been reawakened by global warming and toxic dumping, a nightmare the government tried to keep submerged. Neptune's Reckoning. Terror knows no depth

Bestselling collection

DEAD BAIT

A husband hell-bent on revenge hunts a Wereshark... A Russian mail order bride with a fishy secret... Crabs with a collective consciousness... A vampire who transforms into a Candiru... Zombie piranha...Bait that will have you crawling out of your skin and more. Drawing on horror, humor with a helping of dark fantasy and a touch of deviance, these 19 contemporary stories pay homage to the monsters that lurk in the murky waters of our imaginations. If you thought it was safe to go back in the water... Think Again!

Check out other great

Sea Monster Novels!

Michael Cole

MEGALODON VS COLOSSAL SNAKE

Brought to life by the miracle of DNA cloning, a 93-foot Megalodon shark has escaped captivity. With an insatiable appetite and unmatched aggression, it travels west for the Georgia coast, leaving a path of destruction in its wake. Bullets and harpoons can't penetrate it, steel nets can't hold it, and it's only a matter of time before the whole world finds out about it. In a race to stop the beast, the organization responsible recruit a marine biologist and a herpetologist to develop a plan to catch it. To do it, they must unleash the company's other genetically modified experiment—a 150-foot snake, resurrected from the DNA of the mighty Titanoboa. The pursuit leads to inevitable combat, and the scientists are forced to witness the deadly realities of genetic tampering. As the battle escalates, it is clear nobody is safe...and that nature never intended for these beasts to return. As the destruction mounts, and the death toll climbs, the true loser of Megalodon vs. Colossal Snake is humanity.

Tim Waggoner

TEETH OF THE SEA

They glide through dark waters, sleek and silent as death itself. Ancient predators with only two desires – to feed and reproduce. They've traveled to the resort island of Las Dagas to do both, and the guests make tempting meals. The humans are on land, though, out of reach. But the resort's main feature is an intricate canal system . . . . . . and it's starting to rain.